NOBODY'S BUSINESS

•

Gina Ardito

AVALON BOOKS
NEW YORK

Published by Avalon Books,
an imprint of Thomas Bouregy & Co., Inc.
160 Madison Avenue, New York, NY 10016

Library of Congress Cataloging-in-Publication Data

Ardito, Gina.
  Nobody's business : a nobody romance / Gina Ardito.
      p.   cm.
  ISBN 978-0-8034-7603-5 (hardcover. : alk. paper)   1. Women
skiers—Fiction.   2. Sportswriters—Fiction.   3. Bed and breakfast
accommodations—Fiction.   I. Title.
  PS3601.R43N62 2011
  813'.6—dc22   2011018707

PRINTED IN THE UNITED STATES OF AMERICA
ON ACID-FREE PAPER
BY RR DONNELLEY, BLOOMSBURG, PENNSYLVANIA

For Tori. In my wildest dreams, I couldn't have envisioned a more wonderful daughter. May you always seek out the challenges in life and coast through them with ease.

Author's Note

Although Ski-Hab is the product of my imagination, winter sports rehabilitation programs for the disabled have existed since shortly after World War II and are available worldwide. My research has given me new insight into the courage and determination of the individuals involved, and I thank them for their inspiration.

Chapter One

I bet, in your wildest dreams, you never thought you'd be living with your mother at your age."

Douglas Sawyer glowered at the twenty-something-year-old sports star sprawled in the corner of his white leather sectional. "Is that supposed to be funny, Ace?"

Ace Riordan, snowboarding king, flashed the trademark grin that had catapulted him into million-dollar endorsements and worldwide fame. "Well, yeah. You don't see the humor in this situation?"

With a broad sweep of his arm, he indicated the evidence of Violet Sawyer's complete takeover of what had once been a glorious beacon of successful bachelorhood. Floor-to-ceiling windows overlooking the Manhattan skyline were now marred with whimsical suncatchers to prevent the birds from smacking their little beaks into the glass. The scent of pumpkin pie wafted from lit candles in odd-shaped jars on the mantel above Doug's pristine white marble fireplace. Floral arrangements from his recent hospital stay, some with GET WELL SOON balloons still attached, circled the room. A colorful pile of gossip rags—complete with lurid headlines that screamed about adopted babies, cheating spouses, and the latest celebrities to check into rehab—spread across his glass cocktail table. The top tabloid in the pile featured a smiling couple beneath the banner *April "Reins" In Her Man: Mom & Doc Will Wed!*

The woman in the cover photo caught Doug's attention. Familiarity itched in his brain. Cute, perky-looking, with brownish-red hair and a flashlight-sized diamond sparkling on her finger. Where had he seen that smile before? The crinkled

1

eyes, the dimples, the curve of her lips all tickled some ancient memory from his past.

Mom's laughter trilled from behind the club chair where Doug reclined, his stocking feet on the matching ottoman. "Will you look at that?" she said, her tone filled with wonder. "Isn't that the most adorable thing you've ever seen?"

When he looked up at her, she pointed to the high-definition television. Doug fought back a groan of impatience. Of all the stupid . . .

A squirrel rode water skis around a kiddie pool.

Ever since his discharge from the hospital, his mother had slowly wormed her influence back into his life. The painkillers were to blame, of course. That, and the fact he couldn't stir himself up enough to really care. Earlier, Doug had spent the afternoon in a medicine-induced daze while she watched three hours' worth of soap operas. Which was why he'd welcomed Ace's arrival and its inherent distraction.

"Sweet," Ace commented, and Doug suddenly wished for a muzzle for the kid's grinning mouth.

"Wait," Mom said to both men. "Let me rewind this so you can see it from the beginning."

Doug silently cursed the day his cable company added the ability to stop, rewind, and replay any particular scene on any television show at any given moment. At first he'd considered having a DVR a godsend. As a sports journalist, he loved having the ability to fully analyze a layup, determine if a running back's feet had truly landed flat in the end zone, and ascertain if the ump's called strike should have been a ball four.

Now, however, he glowered at the goofy animal program, and then up at his mother, who hovered nearby, one eye on the television while the other kept watch over him—as if he might explode at any second.

"What happened to the mom who taught high school English and insisted on my reading Tolstoy and Hemingway every night?" he grumbled.

His mother blinked, and her eyes glistened with unshed tears. "She nearly lost her only child in an incident outside of Baghdad." The words, a harsh whisper, grated the air. "And so now she has decided the world doesn't need war to be glamorized quite so much."

"I miss the old mom," he said pointedly.

"And I miss the old son." She bent to ruffle his hair. Good God, did she think he was still ten years old? She flexed her wrist to stare at her watch. "Ooh! It's time for your meds. Ace, why don't you pop in that DVD you brought with you while I get Doug his pills?"

"You brought a DVD?" Doug arched a brow at Ace. "What is this? A date? Want me to leave the room and give you two some alone time?"

When Ace shook his head, his golden curls glistened beneath the jarred candlelight as if he were a star in some shampoo commercial. "The DVD's for you, pal o' mine."

The young man rose, picked up a black case near the mess of tabloids, and strode to the smoked-glass and chrome cabinet. A minute later, the water-skiing squirrel blurred and disappeared, replaced with a blue screen and the directive to hit PLAY.

"Oh, goodie," Doug remarked. "What's in store for us now? A psychic cow? A skateboarding dog? Has the Animal Network found a paint-spitting llama that creates copies of original art masterpieces?"

"You'll find out soon enough." Ace turned from the unit and meandered back to the couch. "Whenever you're ready, Mrs. S.," he called into the kitchen as he resettled himself in his seat.

"What's that supposed to mean?" Doug demanded.

"Lighten up, Dougie." His mother bustled back into the den with a tall glass of water and a handful of pills that she pressed into his left palm. "Here you go."

"Yeah, *Dougie*," Ace repeated in a singsong voice. "Make sure you take your medicine like a good boy so you can be aaaallllll better."

Great. Within an hour of Ace's departure from his apartment, the world would know the age-old nickname that, until now, only his mother dared to use. With sips of water, he swallowed the colorful assortment cupped in his hand. First the blue pill to fight infection. Then the two red caplets to promote healing.

And finally, one of the tiny white ones for pain, which was supposed to give his world a rosy glow. Yeah, right. Like anything in his life would ever be rosy again.

"Any time you're ready to leave, Ace," he growled, "you know where the door is."

"Be quiet and watch," his mother snapped. "This is for your own good." Settling in the matching club chair opposite his, she fumbled for the remote control. With the press of her index finger, she sent the television screen hurtling into a blur of moving shapes.

The speed of the fast-forwarded images merged with the effects of too many meds swimming in his blood. The combination overwhelmed his brain, and he closed his eyes to regain equilibrium, tilting his head into the soft pillow propped against the chair back.

When he finally opened his eyes again, no animals with sporting equipment came into view. Instead, *humans* struggled with sporting equipment. Snowboards and skis.

". . . The program was begun several years ago by a group of local skiers when one of their own arrived home without a limb during the first Gulf War," a male voice-over announced. "Since then, over one hundred injured veterans have found new life on the slopes."

On the giant flat screen, at least a dozen skiers slowly traversed a snowy trail. The camera zoomed closer, and Mom paused the action on a lone figure, gliding downhill in a sit-ski, a quasi-wheelchair mounted on skis.

"It's a rehabilitation program for injured war veterans," Ace elaborated. "I did my community service there."

Ah, yes. His community service. Last year, the snowboarding superstar had been involved in a scuffle at JFK International Airport that resulted in a broken nose for a more virulent member of the press. To help the kid out of what might have been a prison sentence, Doug had written an editorial about the pressure of the pro circuit, the stupidity of the young, and how one mistake shouldn't destroy a promising career. His article didn't score any points from the reporter with the broken nose, but public outcry convinced the New York District

Attorney to settle the case quietly. Ace agreed to enroll in an anger management program and perform four hundred hours of community service.

"Don't say anything yet, Doug," his mother advised. "Just watch." She pressed the PLAY button again, and the screen burst to life.

"The Ski-Hab program is geared to enhance the well-being of our soldiers emotionally, physically, and spiritually. Many of these brave men and women assumed they'd never again lead a normal life until they arrived here at Mount Elsie."

Mount Elsie? Sounded more like a dairy farm than a ski resort. Doug squinted, studying the chairlifts and tree lines, seeking anything that might give him a clue where this mysterious Mount Elsie might be located. Not much to differentiate this place from any other. Lots of snow, chairs on elevated lines scaling higher and higher, the graceful motion of hips and legs creating slaloms down the trails, a rustic two-tiered deck, and picnic tables crowded with people basking in a lemon sun. No gondolas. No flags. No clues that would help him determine what state or country was home for Mount Elsie. He could ask Ace, but that would only lead to his mother thinking he was interested.

On-screen, the reporter interviewed several veterans. One former Marine who had sustained a spinal cord injury admitted he'd suffered from post-traumatic stress until he'd begun the Ski-Hab program.

"I'd lie in that hospital bed and plan how to get my hands on enough pills to end it all," the Marine said.

Doug's skin itched as both his mother and Ace turned hard gazes on him. He returned their scrutiny with a bland expression. "What?"

His mother frowned. "You know what."

"So . . ." He refused to confirm her silent accusation. "What? You want me to write a story about this place? Too late. It's already been done."

"No, Dougie," Mom replied. "You're going to participate."

Oh no. No way. "This is a program for *soldiers*. I'm a reporter."

Okay, he used to be a reporter. Before Iraq. Before he'd embedded with Giles Markham's unit. Before an enemy missile hit their Humvee, killing everyone inside—except him. "Ace pulled some strings and got you enrolled in the Ski-Hab program."

A shot of pain blazed over one shoulder, and he grimaced. "Forget it."

"Not so fast, my son. You owe me. Big time. Who taught you how to throw a curveball? Who was team mom three years in a row when you played peewee football? Who worked summer school to pay for your time at the ice hockey rink?"

"You." Heat washed his nape, and he skimmed a palm down the back of his neck. "All you."

"That's right," she replied with a satisfied smile. "And may I remind you about your crush on that snow bunny when you were fourteen? What was her name again?"

"Brooklyn Raine," he murmured.

Hoots of laughter erupted from Ace. "*You* had a crush on Brooklyn Raine? Oh, my God, that's so chill!"

"That was twenty years ago, for God's sake." Beneath his palm, fine hairs prickled with annoyance. "What's so 'chill' about it?"

"Dude, you have no idea." Ace squirmed in his chair, rising onto his haunches. "So did you, like, write her fan mail and stuff?"

"No," Doug ground out, conveying with that one syllable his refusal to discuss the topic freely.

He hadn't thought about Brooklyn Raine in aeons. While all his high school buddies obsessed about the *Baywatch* babes, he had found his dream girl on the slopes at the World Cup games. Brooklyn Raine had it all: looks, a dynamite personality, and a blinding smile. When she raced in the giant slalom, the sexy swerve of her hips compelled an adolescent boy to stand up and take notice.

"What about later?" Ace pressed. "When you grew up? Did you ever interview her?"

"No."

Ace's denim eyes widened like an eager puppy's. "Too bad.

I bet she would have gone for you. But then again, maybe not. She was married to that Cheviot guy. Did you know Canada named a holiday after him? It's not a bank holiday or anything, but it gives the ski resorts another day to charge higher—"

"Is there a point to this?"

"Not yet." Ace snickered. "But there will be. Do you know I was in kindergarten when Brooklyn Raine won the gold?"

"You're quickly wearing out your welcome, Ace."

"Too bad. I'm not leaving till I get the deets on your great love affair with Brooklyn Raine."

"There was no great love affair."

Yet, by the time he had turned sixteen, his passion for her had grown so manic, he insisted on spending the entire Christmas holiday at the nearest ski mountain on the off chance Brooklyn might appear. Of course, in those days, the nearest ski mountain to their home was a rinky-dink place in West Virginia. A place that had since become a water park based on famous battle sites of the Civil War. A place that a skier of Brooklyn Raine's caliber would *never* visit.

But it was the only ski resort nearby that his single mother could afford. And she'd stretched every penny that holiday season to give Doug the opportunity to learn the sport . . . just in case he should ever meet his dream girl.

"You owe me, Dougie," Mom repeated. "I didn't care what I had to do to get you to the slopes when you were sixteen. Now you'll use those skills to retake control of the life you so casually want to throw away."

"I'm not throwing anything away," he argued. "I couldn't if I wanted to. I threw right-handed, remember?"

Three months ago, when Doug had told his editor he'd give his right arm for an interview with Giles Markham, he'd meant it as a figure of speech.

Fate, however, took him at his word.

Chapter Two

In the kitchen of Snowed Inn Bed-and-Breakfast, Lyn Hill hung up the telephone with an air of defeat.

"T minus ten minutes until their arrival," she told herself with a sigh. "Let the madness begin."

Her sister had come to town, with the entire entourage in tow. Not that she didn't love April and her kids. And April's fiancé struck her as a sensible, caring, responsible guy. Unfortunately, ever since that television stunt featuring April and Jeff, the two had become media darlings.

Her stomach pitched. Even after all these years, the idea of microphones shoved into her face and the glare of flashbulbs left her scared stupid.

Outside, wan December sunlight glinted off the freshly fallen snow coating the windows. Of their own volition, Lyn's toes flexed inside her shoes, as if digging skis into packed powder. She hadn't hit the slopes in three days. And the lack of indulging her favorite outlet wreaked havoc with her nerves.

Maybe when the kids got here, if they weren't too tired from the drive, she could take them over to the mountain for a few runs before the lifts closed.

Leaving the kitchen in the capable hands of her cook, she strode into the parlor. A welcome fire crackled in the natural stone hearth. Cinnamon and cloves, wafting from the hot cider on the sideboard, infused the air with spicy warmth.

Click, clack, squeeeek! Click, clack, squeeeek!

In the ancient rocking chair near the fireplace, Mrs. Bascomb sat with her knitting. The long steel needles slipped through the skein of mint green yarn while she rocked. Looking up, she offered Lyn a serene smile before returning her attention to today's baby blanket project.

Each October, when frosty air swept into their Vermont town, the widow next door brought her rainbow of yarns to Snowed Inn and took her place fireside. Throughout the fall and winter, Mrs. Bascomb and the other knitting club members created change purses, layettes for infants, sweaters and ski hats, home linens, tote bags, and other crafts. During the busier spring and summer months, they'd sell those handmade goodies at country fairs and local shops.

"How soon until your sister and her family arrive?" Mrs. Bascomb asked.

"April just called from the Brown Bear. They'll be here in a few minutes."

The old lady dropped her needles in her lap and smiled reassuringly at Lyn over the top of her square eyeglasses. "Everything's going to be fine, you know."

She offered a grimace as she sank into the matching rocking chair. "I just hope they were able to dodge the paparazzi."

"Honey, I hate to break it to you, but even if some reporter followed them up here, no one's going to care about *you*."

"Gee, thanks a lot."

Mrs. Bascomb's chortles raised hackles on Lyn's nape. "Well, now, you can't have it both ways, Lyn. You wanted anonymity. You got it. You haven't been seen publicly in almost ten years. So at this stage, no one's going to recognize you. Isn't that what you've tried to gain up here?"

Lyn frowned and palmed the fine hairs dancing on the back of her neck. Only someone who'd lived under the fame microscope could understand her fears, her distaste for the invasion of her privacy, the claustrophobic clamor of crowds.

"Lyn?" Mrs. Bascomb's prompt chased away the ghosts. "That is what you want, isn't it? Anonymity?"

"Of course," she replied, her mind still straddling the past and present. A lump rose in her throat, and a quick cough placed her firmly back in the conversation with Mrs. B. "But now, with

April and Jeff in the spotlight, the most rabid reporters are bound to track the lovebirds to my inn. And when they do, they'll put two and two together."

Confusion puckered Mrs. Bascomb's crumpled brow. "Why should they? Your sister's kept mum about you. No one's ever linked her with the once-famous Brooklyn Raine."

Lyn gave her brain a few minutes to process these facts, facts she'd repeated to herself over and over since the day April had told her of the family's vacation plans. "True . . ."

"And I hate to tell you this, but I sincerely doubt those rabid reporters would care any more about you being April's sister except as an interesting side note. You're beyond yesterday's news. You're a dinosaur."

"Once again, thanks a lot."

Dark eyes twinkled behind thick lenses. "I mean it as a compliment, sweetie. You've kept yourself so far below the radar, the public lost interest in you a long time ago." Leaning forward, she patted Lyn's hand in a conciliatory gesture. "Besides, if someone dared to ask nosy questions about you, they'd come up against some mighty high brick walls. The entire town's watching out for you. Your friends and neighbors will make sure to outsiders you're only known as Lyn Hill, proprietor of Snowed Inn, a nice little widow lady who prefers to live like a hermit."

She yanked her hand out of Mrs. Bascomb's reach and tucked her fingers behind her opposing forearm. "I do *not* live like a hermit."

"Mmm-hmm." Mrs. Bascomb sat back, resumed her rocking, gaze now fixed on the rough-hewn crossbeams high overhead. "You know, when you first became involved with this Ski-Hab program, I thought to myself, 'Finally. The Mourning Glory's going to start blooming again.'"

Lyn arched a brow. " 'The Mourning Glory'?"

"Yeah." With a grin, the old lady winked. "You don't know it, but that's the locals' nickname for you."

Acid burned her tongue, and she allowed the sarcasm to drip from her lips. "How complimentary."

"It isn't meant to be a compliment." Mrs. Bascomb pulled

the glasses off her face and chewed on the tip of one side. "It's an observation. Ever since Marc died, you've holed up in this inn like you died too."

"None of you understand," she snapped. "When Marc died, I lost everything. He wasn't just my husband. He was my best friend, my rock, my whole world."

Mrs. Bascomb waved her glasses with a dismissive hand. "Don't invite me to your pity party. I lost my husband too. But I managed to continue living."

"Your husband was seventy and you'd been married for forty-five years when you lost him."

"Which makes it even more devastating. You think your piddly little four-year marriage can compare to a lifetime?"

Beeeeeeeeep! Beep-beep! Beeeeeeeeep!

The sudden eruption of a car horn out front broke the disquiet inside the inn. Relief flooded Lyn's taut skeleton.

"That'll be April and the brood," she announced, forcing a happy air.

"I think I'll see if there are any cookies in the kitchen," Mrs. Bascomb said. "Children love cookies." She rose and, leaving her knitting behind, slipped from the parlor with all the finesse of a snake oil salesman.

Shaking her head to dislodge their conversation, Lyn turned toward the inn's front entrance.

Thump! Thump! Thump!

The familiar, rhythmic thud of visitors stomping snow from their boots echoed in Lyn's pounding heart.

Before she reached the lilac-painted steel door, April flung it open wide, shaking the cranberry wreath hanging outside and allowing a burst of icy air into the overheated room.

"We're here!" she shouted as she sped into the parlor, arms outstretched to engulf Lyn.

Holy happiness, Batman! Lyn had never seen her older sister look so good. A nuclear glow seemed to surround April from head to toe. Her eyes glittered with sparks of light, and her blinding smile illuminated the entire first floor.

"God, Lyn, I'm so happy to see you." She squeezed Lyn tight enough to crack ribs.

"Well, something's made you happy, that's for sure," Lyn replied as she broke the boa constrictor embrace. "But I don't think I can take the credit."

April laughed. "Yeah, it's Jeff, I guess. If I'd have known seeing a psychologist would turn my life around, I would have made an appointment years ago."

"It's not the seeing that's made a difference," a rich baritone said from behind them. "It's the fact the psychologist is crazy in love with you."

One look told Lyn the truth of Jeff's words. The tall, striking man standing in the doorway flashed silver eyes glowing with adoration in her sister's direction. The heat flowing between these two could set the inn ablaze.

The serpent of jealousy wound around Lyn's heart. How did April get so danged lucky?

Shame slammed a spiked heel on the snake's head. Lyn would not begrudge her sister a good, honest, trustworthy man. After all April's trials, she deserved happiness. And thinking of trials . . .

On either side of Jeff stood April's children, Becky and Michael. Luggage surrounded the trio like a fortress.

"Gag me," nineteen-year-old Becky exclaimed with a smirk. "I think I just threw up in my mouth a little."

Jeff's smile only deepened. "Then my work here is done." He ruffled fourteen-year-old Michael's hair. "What about you, sport? Your mom and I nauseate you too?"

"Maybe a little." Michael's gap-toothed grin sent a shiver up Lyn's spine.

She loved her nephew, but sometimes, facing his disability head-on made her squirm. Michael was a child with Down syndrome. And while April had long ago adjusted to his awkward facial features and physical limitations, the rest of the family tended to avoid direct eye contact for fear of hurting the child's feelings with an involuntary wince or grimace.

"Jeff." April dragged Lyn toward the door. "This is my sister, Lyn. Lyn, this is Jeff."

Jeff stepped forward and removed his gloves, tucking them

under his arm. "Brooklyn." He extended a bare hand. Big, warm, gentle hold. Familial. "Nice to meet you. I'm a big fan." With a broad smile, Lyn clasped his fingers. "Same here. And please call me Lyn. I never use my real name anymore. When I was a teenager, a name like Brooklyn Raine set me apart on the racing circuit. Now . . ." Sighing, she shook her head. "It's embarrassing. So for the record, I'm just plain Lyn Hill."

"Hello, hello, nice to meet you too." Becky's sarcastic tone cut in from the doorway. "Can we come inside, please?" She hopped from one foot to the other. "It's freezing out here."

"Whoops! Sorry. That's my fault." Jeff whirled, and after replacing his gloves, stomped to the door to pick up the largest of the three suitcases. Gesturing to the fireplace with its crackling flames, he told the kids, "Go warm yourselves up over there while I drag these inside."

The teenagers thundered into Lyn's parlor, dripping gray slush and trailing white wires attached to earbuds.

"Guys?" April prompted. "Got anything to say to your Aunt Lyn?"

"Yeah. What's there to do around here?" Apparently, Becky missed her mother's veiled hint.

"Guess again," Jeff told her.

When he paired the command with a scathing look, Becky's face flushed.

"Sorry." She stepped forward and embraced Lyn stiffly. "Hi, Aunt Lyn. How are you?"

Approval for Jeff rose a hundred degrees in Lyn's mind. Taking on April's ruffians required a lot of guts, a lot of patience, and a little insanity. To her surprise, Jeff seemed to have reined in both teens and earned their respect in the process. No wonder April raved about him the way she did.

Lyn gave her niece a quick squeeze. "I'm fine, Becs." She released Becky and hugged Michael as well. "I'm glad you guys came. And if you're up for it, I thought we'd hit the slopes while your mom and . . ." She shot a questioning look at April. How should she address Jeff in front of the kids? She doubted they'd call him Dad.

"Jeff," he supplied, as if she'd asked the question aloud. "While your mom and Jeff are getting everything settled," she finished. "Your gear is in the locker room, all ready for you." Michael's slanted eyes widened, and his mouth grew slack with his excitement as he nodded vigorously. Drool spotted the corner of his lip, and Lyn stifled the urge to wipe it away.

"Sure," Becky said. "Think there'll be any cute guys out there today?"

April laughed. "It's a ski resort, Becky. There are cute guys there every day." She wagged a finger. "Just be careful. Some of those ski bums can steal your heart if you let them."

Lyn's gaze swerved from the excited teens to the adults. "Is it okay with you two?"

"Why not?" April replied. "I'm sure we can find some way to pass the time while you're gone." Another heated look passed between April and Jeff, a look so passionate, the serpent around Lyn's heart squeezed her breathless.

"Come on," Lyn murmured to the teenagers. "Let's get our gear and hit the snow."

Chapter Three

No one played the guilt card better than Violet Sawyer. Mere days after Ace's visit—or the "gang shanghai," as he liked to call that afternoon—Doug strapped on, for the first time, the prosthetic arm the hospital had created for him. According to his doctor, the latex and metal contraption was state of the art. But it still looked like what it was: a robotic arm. He might as well start wearing an eye patch and a parrot on his shoulder. At least one day a year he'd look like everyone else—on Halloween.

And how in God's name could he type with this . . . this . . . claw?

But his physical therapist didn't expect him to simply type. No, the torture king wouldn't rest until Doug could feel the difference between the ace of hearts and the jack of clubs with his fake fingers.

Which wasn't going to happen anytime soon.

Although nerves in his upper chest were rewired to control the apparatus, the simplest actions, like raising his hand, took focus and time he'd never needed before that miserable day in Iraq. Tasks he'd done since toddlerhood—tying his shoes, buttoning his shirt, writing his name—had to be relearned in excruciating therapy sessions.

And now, he was about to attempt downhill skiing. With the torture king's blessing, of course.

Mount Elsie, a small ski resort in the middle of Vermont's Green Mountains, catered to local residents, families with small children, and maimed veterans who sought a shot at regaining independence after losing a limb or two. Or three. Or four.

"All set, Doug?"

From his seat on the bench at the bottom of the bunny hill's J-bar, Doug glanced up at his ski instructor, then turned a furious gaze toward Ace. "Is this a joke?"

Kerri-Sue Parker looked exactly the way Doug would expect a Kerri-Sue Parker to look. Perky, blond, blue-eyed, no older than twenty-five, tops. Jeez, he probably owned clothes older than this kid.

Despite her youth, or maybe because of it, she flashed him a blinding smile. "You've got a problem with me, Doug?"

"Yeah," Ace replied with an amused snort. "You're not Brooklyn Raine."

"Who?" Her expression blanked.

Good God, was she younger than he thought? How could anyone even remotely linked to the skiing industry not know the name Brooklyn Raine? Not that there was any truth to Ace's comment. The kid had harped on Doug's teenage crush since the night he'd first learned about it.

"Brooklyn Raine was a slalom skier from the eighties and nineties," Ace told Kerri-Sue with an exaggerated sneer. "You know. The old days. When snowboarding was reserved for the far side of the mountain."

When Ace pointed past the tree line, Kerri-Sue's gaze naturally followed. "Oh. Right." She gave him a thumbs-up. "Got it now."

Thwap! Thwap! Ace bounced on his purple and green board, a subtle hint he was bored and eager to hit whatever challenging slope he could find far from the beginner's area.

"You may not believe this, Doug," he said between bounces, "but you got the best instructor in the program. Kerri-Sue gets results from the troops the other guys can't."

Flashing another dazzling smile, Kerri-Sue shrugged. "It's a gift."

The dawn of understanding illuminated Doug's brain. Of course Kerri-Sue got results. No red-blooded American male would risk disappointing this beautiful snow angel. Except him.

"I want someone else." The meanest, ugliest bulldog on the instructional team. Someone who wouldn't giggle every time he lost his balance and fell on his face.

"Too bad." Kerri-Sue knocked bits of errant snow from her bindings by tapping her pole against her ski. The slow precision in the motion made him think she wished she was pounding his head. "You're stuck with me today. Don't make me knock you on your butt in front of all these Marines."

He took a look around, at the wounded men and women, all struggling to adapt to a new normal. How in God's name had he arrived here? A year ago, he'd had a successful career, a modicum of celebrity in New York journalistic circles, and two working, matching arms. Now he was just another freak in this snow circus.

"You're all in the same boat, Doug," Kerri-Sue added, as if she'd read his thoughts. "We tend to group our students by category. So everyone here this week is a two-tracker with upper torso issues."

"Two-tracker?"

"Yeah," Ace replied from his left. "That means you'll use two skis." He grinned, no doubt proud to show what he'd learned while serving his public penance here.

Kerri-Sue shooed Ace toward the main chairlifts. "Go play, Ace. Doug and I will be fine without you."

Ace turned toward the larger part of the mountain, then back to Doug. "You're sure?"

"Go," Doug replied. One know-it-all youth watching his every move would be all his cracked pride could take during this debacle.

Lucky for him, the kid needed no further prodding. With a whoop of delight, he picked up his board and raced to the main lift line.

Kerri-Sue sighed dramatically. "Alone, at last." She stepped into her skis with a *click-click*. "Basically, we handle five different types of skiers here: two-trackers like you; three-trackers are one-leg amputees who use one ski but two outriggers. An outrigger's that long-handled thing—kinda looks like a pole with the front piece of a ski tacked on."

Doug nodded. He'd seen them before in competition use at the Special Olympics and Disabled Sports games.

"Four-trackers use two skis and two outriggers. Then there's the sit-trackers who work a sit-ski. And visually impaired skiers use a guide. We've got one guy, Max, suffers from some rare vision disorder—he gets, like, tunnel vision and can't see what's on either side of him. He skis with his dog."

Deep inside his brain, a dormant instinct sparked. His reporter's senses tingled, like Spiderman's. But he shoved the sensation away. His reporting days were over; he couldn't type and no way he'd be seen on television with The Claw. "Yeah, right."

"No joke. He's got a human guide for racing and stuff, but just for toodling around the easy slopes, he uses his Labrador retriever. The dog's a two-tracker, by the way."

A smile twitched his lips, and Kerri-Sue beamed brighter than sunshine on fresh snow. "Now that's more like it. You're actually a good-looking guy when you're not growling at me."

"I'm old enough to be your father." Or, at least, an uncle.

She gave him the critical once-over. "You think so? You're . . . what? Thirty-five?"

He shrugged. Thirty-five in years, but ninety in experience. And feeling older every minute . . .

"How old do you think *I* am?"

A dangerous question. And he had no intention of stepping closer to *that* ledge. Not with a woman who could push him off a cliff and get away with it.

"Come on," Kerri-Sue pressed. "You started this. Finish it." He'd lowball her to be on the safe side. "Twenty-one."

She laughed. "Now you're just making fun of me. Come on, be honest. I can take it. How old do you really think I am?"

"No more than twenty-six."

"Which would make you too young to be my father. The fact is, though, I'll be forty this coming August." She must have seen his eyes widen because she nodded like a bobblehead doll. "Really. Good Swedish genes. *Great* Swedish genes, actually."

Okay, so maybe he didn't have clothes older than her. But maybe she only told him she was almost forty to make him feel better somehow. Some kind of pity-lie for the cripple. His doubts must have shown on his face because she leaned closer, eyes crinkled with mirth. "Wanna see my driver's license?"

Embarrassment crept up his nape, and he quickly looked away, focusing on the J-bar lift as it revolved from the bottom to the top of the slope.

"I can go back to the locker room and get my wallet," she persisted.

Leveling a steely gaze her way, he replied, "I'll take your word for it."

"Good. Then slap on your helmet and let's get started." She picked up the helmet and shoved it at Doug's chest.

Instinctively, he reached with his right arm, but, of course, nothing happened. He'd left his prosthesis in his slopeside condo. Still not one hundred percent comfortable with the motion of the fake arm, he preferred to relearn skiing without it.

"Here." With a maternal sigh, Kerri-Sue slipped the helmet over Doug's head, then slid the goggles into place over his face. She bent close to study his field of vision. "Can you see okay?"

He had to swallow hard to keep his pride from screaming that he could do these tasks himself. Because, the truth of the matter was, he couldn't. Too frustrated to speak, he settled for a nod.

Apparently that was enough acknowledgment for Kerri-Sue. With gentle fingers, she clipped the strap under his chin.

Once again, he gulped back his resentment. Good God, how many more insults would his ego have to suffer? How on earth could he ever be whole again? Bitterness bubbled like bile in his gut. He couldn't. The best he could hope for was a half-existence. He'd either be stuck fumbling with that phony artifice that masqueraded as a human arm or playing helpless victim so others could tie his shoes for him.

No. No way. He'd fight this battle. No way did he intend to spend the rest of his life with a hired coddler. Or his mother.

Kerri-Sue smiled, her cheeks rosy from the cold. "Come on, Doug. Let's hit the slopes!"

After leaving Becky and Michael under the watchful eyes of the kitchen staff amid steaming cups of cocoa and squares of brownies, Lyn took one of her last runs of the day. At the top of the Snow Blind trail's final hill, she stopped to watch the new Ski-Hab recruits on the bunny slope, Snow Wonder.

One by one, with their instructors alongside them for guidance, the class of two-trackers eased their way down the graduated hill in the classic S pattern. Nice. Slow. Steady form.

The good thing about Marines: they knew how to take orders.

On an inhale of crisp mountain air, she swooped closer to the beginner's area. Years of skiing this mountain had made her all too familiar with the instructors. These days, she could recognize any staff member based on his or her unique motions on the slopes.

Curiosity riveted her to the student working with Kerri-Sue. The slender, beauty-queen blond, usually the most popular and successful of the instructors, struggled with a hulking, one-armed giant of a man.

As he attempted the winding slalom downhill, his center of gravity tilted, and he faltered on the skis. *Splat!* He landed hard on his right side—the side without an arm. Rather than flipping to his left and regaining his stance, he began the wiggle routine, which Lyn usually associated with children and weaker amputees.

At first, Kerri-Sue stood back and watched, patiently waiting for him to realize his mistake and correct his approach. But as he continued to flounder while she no doubt stiffened in her boots, she finally broke protocol and bent to wrap an arm around him.

Oh, for heaven's sake. The bigger they were, the more they acted like babies. This one was no exception. Time for her to intervene.

One strong push with her poles set her in motion, and she quickly gathered enough speed to cross the flat section that separated her trail from the bunny slope. Kerri-Sue must have heard her approach, because her head jerked up toward the crest of the hill. Seconds later, the instructor dropped her hold on the student and stood upright, hands at her sides.

Lyn came to a hard stop, spraying snow on the man's black ski pants. "Back off, Kerri-Sue," she said, planting her poles deep enough into the ground to keep them upright. "I've got this one." She turned to the man whose face was hidden behind a helmet and snow goggles. "What's your name, soldier?" she barked with the force of a drill sergeant.

"Umm . . . Lyn . . ." Kerri-Sue leaned toward her.

Lyn waved her off, never turning her gaze from the man on the frozen ground.

"No, Lyn, really," Kerri-Sue continued in a hurried hush. "You need to know—"

"I'm talking to the soldier now, Kerri-Sue. Go wait for us at the lift, please."

"I'm not a soldier," the man ground out through gritted teeth.

Huh? Lyn started. "You're not?" Confusion smeared across her brain like petroleum jelly, and she turned to Kerri-Sue for clarity.

Kerri-Sue's cheeks reddened with embarrassment, but her eyes blazed outrage. "Doug is our first civilian in the program. He was referred to us by Ace Riordan. *Remember?*" She edged the last word with frozen iron.

Oops.

Vaguely, Lyn recalled the program's director, Richie Armstrong, telling her about a prospective recruit—a civilian— who'd been injured in some kind of accident. When Richie had confided the guy was a friend of Ace's, Lyn had hesitated to agree. No one had bothered to tell her the civilian had been accepted, without her approval.

Oh, she liked Ace—most of the time. But Ace had a reckless streak. Which made him an ideal athlete. Not, however, the most reliable participant in a program like Ski-Hab. And this was a friend of Ace's. What were the chances the man would take the work involved seriously enough to succeed? She'd purposely limited Ski-Hab to members of the armed forces because they were in excellent physical condition and accustomed to following orders.

Still . . .

Ace's time with Ski-Hab must have left a positive mark for him to refer their first civilian. A civilian who currently flopped on the snow like a fish pulled out of an ice hole. While she played Attila the Hun, snapping demands.

"My apologies, Mr. . . . ?"

"Sawyer," he replied through the same barely moving lips. "Doug Sawyer."

Once again, Lyn turned her attention to Kerri-Sue. "Go wait at the lift."

While Kerri-Sue pushed off toward the rest of the class, the man on the ground struggled with the length of his skis, fumbling to turn himself around.

"Have you ever skied before, Mr. Sawyer?"

She'd softened her tone, but if the glare he shot in her direction was an indication, he'd snow ski with Satan before he forgave her.

"With one arm?" he retorted. "No."

"I mean, ever. One arm or two."

"Yes."

Good. Thank God. "So you remember how to get up when you fall down, right?"

"Yeah, but I'm at a disadvantage since I have no arm on this side to use for support."

"Then you'll have to flip yourself around to the side that has an arm, won't you?"

"You could lend a hand, you know."

"I could," she agreed, and folded her arms over her chest. "But that would defeat the purpose of Ski-Hab. Now flip."

He struggled, but managed to face the other way, positioning his skis parallel and facing upward. Pole planted firmly, he pulled himself to a standing position. Thunderous applause and cheers erupted from the circle of people standing on the sidelines.

At last, the man turned to face Lyn, a relieved grin splitting his cheeks below the bridge of his goggles.

"Well done, Mr. Sawyer." She clapped her gloved hands in muted applause. "How do you feel?"

"Better," he said.

"Ready to do it again?" she asked.

"Yeah."

"Good." With one quick shove against his armless shoulder, she knocked him off-balance.

He teetered for the briefest moment, and then fell right back into the same patch of snow he'd just managed to escape.

"Do it again."

Chapter Four

Michael had disappeared.

Becky stood near their empty table in the lodge and swore softly. She'd told him to stay put while she took a quick trip to the ladies room downstairs. But did he listen to her? *Of course not.*

Around her, groups of people milled, packing up gear, drying wet garments on the coin-operated bootwarmers, and making plans for the evening. Kids shouted for one last cup of hot cocoa before the employees closed down the cafeteria area.

But not Michael.

She peered through the scratchy window of what passed as the resort's arcade room, with its ancient pinball machine and lone combination–Pac-Man/Ms. Pac-Man/Tetris game.

No Michael.

Okay, don't panic. He's done this before.

With deep, calming inhales, she noted her brother's gloves neatly framing his empty cocoa cup. His jacket, helmet, and goggles covered the orange Formica windowsill overlooking the outdoor deck. Which meant he hadn't gone outside.

A lot of people mistook Michael's disability for stupidity. But children with Down syndrome weren't stupid. Most of them were simply slower to develop than other children their age. In a nutshell, they had the sense to come in out of the rain—or snow, in this case. No way Michael would have wandered outside without his coat and gloves. The kid was too smart for that.

So where would he have gone? To look for Aunt Lyn? Maybe. But if he'd wanted to find their aunt, he knew how to notify her. All ski lifts had phones in the booths at the top and bottom of the hills. Chalkboards outside were used to alert skiers to possible emergencies such as lost children, lift closures, or sudden incoming storms.

Becky's first stop, then, should be the information desk. She trudged over to the dim alcove beside the game room, her boots heavy as lead on her feet. The woman in the traditional Mount Elsie uniform of burgundy and gold shirt with burgundy pants was currently helping a man wearing a—holy cow—full-length silver fur coat!

From the snippets of overheard conversation, she concluded he wanted to change his one-day lift ticket into a multi-day.

On a deep sigh, Becky shifted her weight to one hip and rubbed the tight knot in her thigh. God, her legs were cramped! Unlike Aunt Lyn, she didn't spend every frosty day conquering the slopes. And now she paid the price for too much time playing that stupid bunny game on her laptop instead of getting a little more physical exercise. Evie, her track-star dorm mate, would probably groove on seeing her now.

Once she got back to the inn this afternoon, she'd head straight outside for a soak in the hot tub. Of course, first, she had to figure out where her brother had wandered off to.

While she waited her turn in line, she studied the counter littered with colorful pamphlets for local inns, hotels, and restaurants. Corkboard walls held push-pinned photos of gorgeous tree-enclosed ski chalets available for weekly or monthly rental, advertisements for horse-drawn sleigh or dogsled rides, a giant trail map, and postcards of the nearby mountain vistas. In a corner behind the counter stood a milk crate overflowing with scarves, hats, and single gloves, marked LOST AND FOUND.

Well, at least she'd come to the right place.

"What do you mean, you'll only credit me eighty percent?" The man in the fur coat clamped his fingers onto the edge of the counter and leaned forward, his bald head jutting out like a cannonball from his neck.

The woman behind the counter—Jill, according to her burgundy and gold nametag—went into her company policy script.

A needle of sympathy stabbed Becky's nerve endings. Three years of retail customer service experience gave her a pretty good inkling what Jill would have liked to say instead of the blah-blah-blah management forced her to spew. Any guy wearing a full-length fur coat certainly wouldn't starve over the twenty-dollar difference.

"I want to see a manager," the man insisted.

Naturally. Right on cue. Because she was in a rush.

Despite the cramps and exhaustion creeping up her legs, she stamped her foot—not hard, but apparently loud enough for the two people at the information counter to hear; they then swerved their attention her way.

"Sorry," she murmured.

After enduring an icy glare from Mr. Fur Coat, Jill picked up the intercom to page the lodge manager. Becky stifled another sigh. If she planned to find Michael before spring, she'd be better off without any help from the information booth.

Turning, she opted to ask the staff members who were currently cleaning and scrubbing the lunch tables. Unfortunately, after stopping every pimple-faced mountain geek in range—and surviving the pungent odor of stale French fries they seemed to wear like expensive cologne—Becky remained clueless.

No one remembered seeing Michael. No surprise, really. With the crowds inside this place, who would remember one insignificant kid in a navy blue turtleneck and black ski pants?

Another quick glance at the info counter where the guy in the fur coat still fumed and shouted about his lousy twenty bucks. Shoot. Aunt Lyn would be back any minute. If she didn't find Michael soon, she'd have to call Mr. Armstrong to put out an APB. And then Aunt Lyn would freak. The minute they got home, she'd tell Mom. And Jeff. Becky shivered.

Jeff already thought she was a screwup. Not that he ever came right out and said anything. Oh no. He was far too professional for that. But every time she did something he didn't like, he got this look on his face, like he'd just swallowed drain cleaner.

Like earlier, when she'd asked Aunt Lyn what there was to

do around here. It was *supposed* to be a joke. Everybody should have known she was kidding. They'd come up every winter for the last five years. She knew what there was to do. But Jeff had leaped all over her with his "Guess again," and she wound up apologizing like a four-year-old. Over a joke! Now, if her soon-to-be-stepfather found out Michael had wandered off on her watch, she'd be branded a loser for all time.

She drew in a deep breath. Okay. He hadn't gone outside. And he wasn't in the lunchroom. The only other nearby area was the bar. Yeah, right. Totally doubtful.

The locker room? With his gear still here? Nope. Not likely.

Downstairs? A good possibility. Between the ski store with its varied array of snow toys, and the restrooms, there were plenty of reasons for Michael to head downstairs. Since she'd expected him to wait up here, she could have easily walked right past him on the lower level and never noticed.

Time for a quick U-turn. With silent pleas that she'd find him below, Becky gripped the wooden rail and clumsily thumped down the stairs. Three steps from the bottom, she stopped and scanned the numerous heads of the people milling around the lower floor. Snippets from a hundred different conversations echoed in the beige-bricked hall. A quick glance over the people seated on the scarred wooden benches on either side of the staircase brought no relief.

Please, Michael. Please be here somewhere.

And suddenly, there he was—not on a bench, but walking in the crowd. His pale face and wet eyes glowed ghostly beneath the overhead florescent lights. Guilt pounded her conscience like a jackhammer. He looked scared to death.

Your fault, the hammer drummed. *Your fault, your fault, your fault . . .*

She raised a hand, but before she could gain his attention, Michael turned to look behind him. She tracked his gaze and spotted a guy pushing his way through the clusters of people, intent on, in Becky's opinion, keeping Michael in his sights.

Who was that creep? Familiarity tickled her memory. She'd seen him somewhere before; she was almost positive. She narrowed her eyes and stared harder at the approaching blond man. Where had she seen his face?

Probably on one of those news programs that trap kiddie predators.

She veered her attention back to Michael in time to catch him ducking into the ski shop on his right.

Good boy. Stay with the ski staff. I'll take care of your stalker.

With heavy thumps, Becky descended the last steps and plodded to the store's entrance. She hit the doorjamb a boot step before her target.

"Hold it right there!" she shouted. With her arms spread so her fingers could clutch either side of the doorway, she blocked him from moving past her. "That's my brother you're stalking, so back off. Now."

To her surprise, he burst out laughing. "That's a new one." He took a step closer.

"I mean it. Back off." Arms still creating a barrier, Becky shouted over her shoulder, "Somebody call the cops."

People inside and outside the shop stopped in mid-conversation to stare at Becky, the stranger, and Michael. A murmur of interest rippled through the crowd.

"Becky!" Michael exclaimed. "Stop! You're embarrassing me."

"You think I care?" she demanded, her iciest stare fixed on the cretin, who seemed more amused than intimidated.

His lake blue eyes twinkled with some secret, which really stiffened her spine. He was younger than she'd originally assumed. Older than her, but definitely under thirty. His scruffy jaw flexed as he tossed his shoulder-length golden hair with a graceful flick of his hand. Her heart went into overdrive. God, what a shame.

Belying the tingles of attraction warming her insides, she turned to the dozens of people watching the drama unfold. "Take a good look at this guy," she announced loudly. "Post his picture all around the resort so he can't try to kidnap someone else."

"My picture's already plastered all over the resort," he replied, his voice melodious in its velvet tones. His self-deprecating grin rekindled a spark of memory inside her brain. Was it true? Did he really have his image tacked up all over Mount Elsie? Why else would he look so familiar to her?

The guy held up his hands in a gesture of surrender. "I'm Ace Riordan. You know, the Aerial Snowball?"

Ace Riordan. Oh, my God.

Fire bloomed in her face up to her hairline.

Pass the butter. I'm toast.

Thoughts of homicide sizzled through Doug's brain as he stared up at the villainess intent on torturing him. "Well, Mr. Sawyer?" Her soft voice contradicted any lupine characteristics. "Shall we make a mogul out of you? Or do you think you can get up on your own?"

A mogul? The skier's version of a speed bump? Forget wolf. This woman was pure coyote. So why didn't any of the instructors chase her out of here? Set some kind of trap for her?

Well, if no one else would engage in this battle, he'd have to take care of it himself. But first, he wanted to get up—to face her on an even keel. Once again, he flipped to his left side, set his skis across the incline, and slammed his pole into the ground to support himself. He struggled, but managed to rise with a little more ease than he had on his first attempt.

His gaze hot enough to melt all the snow within five square miles, he faced his adversary. She was über-petite, a full foot or more shorter than his own six-foot-three-inch frame. And he outweighed her by at least a hundred pounds. Her face, from the bridge of the nose up, was hidden behind a black helmet and pink-tinted goggles.

She grinned—blinding, sweet, joyous—and words flew around his head like birds around the Cheshire cat.

"Congratulations, Mr. Sawyer. You've conquered the highest peak you'll have to face—Mount Self-Pity. Now, go join your comrades. Good luck to you."

Picking up her poles, she pushed off on the *schuss-schuss-schuss* of skis on flat terrain.

Surprise left him slack-jawed. He stood alone, watching the woman glide toward the lodge area. When she reached the outdoor deck, she stepped out of her skis, locked them on a rack, and climbed the stairs.

"Doug?" Kerri-Sue's voice came from beside him. Somehow, she'd slipped close while he'd been distracted. "You ready for another run?"

His focus, however, still remained glued to the place where the mystery skier had disappeared. "Who was that?"

Kerri-Sue turned toward the lodge, then back to Doug with a careless shrug. "Lyn? She's just one of the locals. Owns a bed-and-breakfast in town."

He arched a brow. "And you take direction from the local innkeeper?"

"Huh?" Her expression blanked.

"The minute she showed up and said something, you scattered. Why?"

She laughed. "Come on." With a wave of her ski pole, she indicated the lift where a dozen people milled about. "The rest of the team is waiting."

After fifteen years as a reporter, Doug knew a brush-off when he heard one. Once again, a tingle rippled through him, his sixth sense suspecting a deeper, more interesting story. And once again, he squelched the instinct to press for details. Those adrenaline-crazed days of chasing down leads—racing from airport to airport, standing in feverish crowds where the frenzy grew contagious—were long gone. Armless reporters need not apply.

He shook off the self-pity. In that respect, the Coyote was absolutely right. If he had any intention of regaining a shadow of the man he'd been before Iraq, he needed to stop feeling sorry for himself. His gaze studied the group near the lift.

Among the students sharing Doug's class was a female lance corporal who'd lost both hands thanks to third-degree burns from an IED. Her fiancé had told her he didn't care if she couldn't carry a bouquet at their wedding. He planned to marry *her,* not her hands. But that wasn't good enough for a woman who'd climbed so high in the United States Marine Corps before the age of twenty-three. With eight months until her big day, she'd enrolled in Ski-Hab to master every skill that came naturally to any two-handed woman, from holding a bouquet to cooking a five-course meal to cradling an infant. A nineteen-year-old had lost his right arm thanks to a lucky shot that penetrated his body armor. Nineteen. Cripes. When Doug was nineteen, the biggest tragedy facing him had been whether he'd pass his English Lit class. After Ski-Hab, this kid planned to attend law school. His dream was to become an attorney specializing in rights for the disabled.

If his classmates, despite their youth and the horrors they'd seen, could overcome their adversities, Doug refused to surrender to any weakness of his own.

"I'm ready," he said gruffly. "Let's go."

One quick push, and he glided toward the Marines and their respective instructors.

"Hey, who was that?" Private First Class Logan Randall, future lawyer, pointed in the direction the Coyote had skied.

"I have no idea," Doug grumbled.

"Yeah?" Lance Corporal Chrissy Scott, future bride, replied. "If that's how a total stranger treats you, I'd hate to spend Christmas at your house."

"Oh, well then I'll scratch your name off the guest list." He scanned the curious stares facing him, and discomfort itched beneath his collar. "Are we gonna ski or what?"

"We're gonna ski!" Sergeant Ramon Henriquez announced.

On boisterous cheers, the Marines lined up, Doug somewhere in the middle, and prepared to conquer Snow Wonder and its J-bar ski lift one more time.

Chapter Five

Once inside the ski lodge, Lyn was headed toward the employees' lounge on the lower level when Becky's strident shout ripped through her.

Post his picture all around the resort so he can't try to kidnap someone else.

Fear slammed her chest like a concrete wall. Michael. Dear God, had someone tried to kidnap Michael?

In her heavy ski boots, running was impossible. Thanks to years of practiced experience, she flipped the buckles on both boots from the calf to the top of her foot in one rapid motion. She pulled the shell apart and yanked her feet out one at a time. Abandoning the empty boots, Lyn raced in her thermal socks to the ski shop. She hit the rear doorway at top speed, zigzagged past the racks of rental skis, and came to a dead stop at a cluster of slack-jawed employees.

"Michael!" she gasped. "Where's Michael?"

"Right here, Aunt Lyn." He stepped into her line of vision, clearly confused by all the chaos. He blinked several times—his doe eyes wide and teeth chewing his lower lip.

Lyn's gaze veered from her nephew to her niece. In contrast to Michael's puzzlement, Becky sported bright pink cheeks and a fighter's stance. Her eyes, however, sat shielded behind heavy lids. She stood in the shop's main entrance, hands fisted at her sides, chest heaving as if she'd just raced the giant slalom.

Beyond Becky, Ace Riordan loitered in the hall, the insipid grin he wore after every first-place finish splitting his cheeks.

"Hey, Lyn," he greeted her with a quick nod. "How's it going? These two characters with you?"

"Ace." Lyn slowly took in the scene, but she couldn't figure out exactly what she'd walked into. "They're my niece and nephew. What's going on?"

"I'm clueless," he drawled.

"I'll tell you what's going on!" Becky exclaimed. "He was stalking my brother."

Ace shot up his hands. "Whoa. No stalking. Honest. I found him outside the men's room crying. If you really cared so much, maybe you should have kept a closer watch on him instead of letting him wander around all alone."

Becky, tears glistening in her eyes, turned to Lyn. "He was supposed to stay upstairs. I just went to the ladies' room, Aunt Lyn. Honest. I came back, and he was gone."

"You took too long," Michael added. "And I had to go too."

With Becky's attention placed squarely between Lyn and Michael, Ace stepped inside the ski shop. "I tried to help the kid, but he said he's not allowed to go anywhere with strangers." He bobbed his head in Michael's direction. "He decided on his own to head to the ski shop. Said they'd page his aunt and his sister. Smart boy."

Becky planted her hands on her hips. "So then why were you following him?"

"To make sure no one else hassled him!"

"No one *else*," Becky stressed. "Meaning you'd already hassled him."

Lyn allowed her gaze to scour the room. All the employees in the ski shop seemed glued to the scene unfolding before them rather than returning to their work. "Hold up," she said to the three young people. "Let's take this somewhere quieter, okay? Follow me."

"But—" Becky began.

Lyn cut her off with a quick air karate chop.

In heavy silence, she led them back past the rental skis, through the rear door, and into the dim hallway where her boots still sat. Pausing only long enough to scoop them up, she strode along the cracked linoleum floor. The *thump-thump* of snow-board boots echoed from those who trailed behind her. She reached the entrance to the employee lounge and pushed the door open with a hint of caution.

Dark and empty.

Flipping on the lights, she ushered the rest of the players inside with a sweep of her hand. "Everybody take a seat." She gestured to a long gray table surrounded by blue plastic chairs.

On the screech of metal on tile, the trio did as she asked. Lyn remained standing, the position of power. "Ace," she said, "what are you doing in Vermont? Don't you have a Canadian competition coming up?"

He stole a heated glance toward Becky, but his intensity dimmed as he looked up at Lyn. "I put the games on hold. I've got a friend in Ski-Hab."

"Oh, right," Lyn replied without thinking. "Mr. Sawyer."

He arched a brow. "You met him?"

Funny, Ace sounded panicked at the idea. "Why?" She cocked her head, studied him. "Is that a problem?"

"Nope." His posture relaxed, and he stared at his fingernails. "How's Doug doing?"

"Struggling." Her mind flashed on the image of Mr. Sawyer flopping in the snow, followed by the anger in his eyes when he rose a second time. "But he'll get the hang of it eventually, I'm sure. How do you know him?"

"He didn't tell you?"

"I was assisting with his rehabilitation, not serving tea and chitchat."

Ace grinned, his teeth practically nuclear with their white glow. "Oh, well, he and I go way back. He helped me out with that little legal issue at the airport."

"Yeah?" Becky's sarcastic edge sliced into the conversation. "You harass kids in airports too?"

Lyn's focus shifted from Becky to Ace and back again. Sparks flew between these two brighter than Fourth of July fireworks. Best to break this up before someone got hurt. Knowing each of the combatants as well as she did, Lyn considered them well-matched, but far too young to handle the heat they'd engender.

Much to her relief, Ace glanced at his watch. "In fact, lessons should be just about over. I think I'll go meet Doug in the training center."

"I think that's an excellent idea," Lyn said evenly.

Inside his slope-side condominium unit, Doug collapsed into a leather recliner with an icy beer and the television remote control. He clicked the on button and scanned through the available channels, finally settling on a local news program.

While the bland, blond weatherman forecasted another perfect ski day for tomorrow, Ace, phone to his ear, called out from the kitchen area. "Mushroom and pepperoni okay with you?"

"Yeah, sure."

After placing the order with the local pizzeria, Ace dropped the receiver on the table and bounced onto the couch next to Doug's chair, propping his stocking feet on the coffee table. "It'll be about an hour for delivery. Giorgio's must be cranking tonight."

"Whatever." Exhaustion had a bigger claim on Doug than hunger.

He took a swig of the beer, let the cool liquid sluice down his parched throat. God, he ached everywhere. Even his missing arm felt battered and bruised from the exertion of the day. He'd strapped on his prosthesis when he'd reached the condo. Oh sure. His nerves sent twinges from his shoulder to work his fake arm. Still, the pain he felt had nothing to do with impulses. *Phantom pain,* the medical team called the phenomenon. But there was nothing phantom about it. No doubt doctors came up with the term to discourage amputees from mourning their loss.

"So." Ace pointed his amber bottle toward Doug. "How was your first actual day on the slopes? Anything interesting happen?"

"I got bruises on my butt." Doug set his beer on the table beside him and leaned forward, his hand moving to the waistband of his pants. "Wanna see?"

Eyes wide with mock panic, Ace slid away to the farthest corner of the couch. "Dude. No. You are totally delusional.

I'm talking about your rendezvous with your longtime sweetheart."

With an easy grin, Doug picked up his beer. "What longtime sweetheart?"

"Brooklyn."

"Brooklyn Raine?" Doug laughed. "Oh, right. *I'm* delusional." He tilted the bottle toward his mouth.

"No, seriously. I ran into her in the lodge. She said she worked with you today."

The beer collided with a gasp of surprise in his throat, and Doug choked. "Brooklyn Raine?" he repeated on a rasp.

"Yeah. You met her, didn't you? She said you were"—Ace pitched his voice higher—" 'struggling, but he'll eventually get the hang of it.' "

Doug's mind scrambled to catch up to the conversation. When had Brooklyn Raine worked with him? He must have misunderstood. Either that, or the single beer had already gone to his head. "Let me get this straight. You ran into Brooklyn Raine. Here."

Surely he would have recognized her. But the only people he'd worked with today were Kerri-Sue . . .

And the Coyote.

His stomach pitched as realization swirled his insides.

"Yes, Brooklyn Raine. Yes, here." Ace cocked his head, peered at him through narrowed eyes. "Are you okay?"

Doug swallowed hard. "You mean the coyote Kerri-Sue claimed was a nice, friendly innkeeper named Lyn was Brooklyn Raine?"

Of course she was. Crazy as it might sound, the idea actually made sense when he considered the big picture.

"Coyote?" Ace sat up and slid his feet to the floor. "What coyote? What happened on the slopes today?"

Briefly, Doug explained about his run-in with the mystery skier named Lyn, leaving out, of course, that she'd shoved him back to the ground. His ego couldn't take another blow today.

Ace grinned. "Yep. That definitely would have been Brooklyn. She's the driving force behind the whole Ski-Hab program, though only the insiders know it."

"Which explains why Kerri-Sue took direction from her," Doug concluded. "But what I don't understand is why Kerri-Sue denied knowing who Brooklyn was in the first place."

Ace's face blanked. "Huh?"

"Remember? This morning? When you went into your diatribe about snowboarders getting no respect?"

"Oh, right." Ace took a long sip of beer, swallowed. "They're all like that around here. The town makes sure no one knows who Lyn is . . . or, technically, I guess, *was.* You ask anybody in this whole *state,* they've never heard of Brooklyn Raine. *Lyn Hill,* on the other hand, is the sweet little lady who runs Snowed Inn, a quaint bed-and-breakfast on the outskirts of town. Which reminds me. I probably should have warned you. Lyn has no clue about how you came to be injured or what you used to do before . . ." He gestured to Doug's right shoulder. "You know."

"Before I lost my arm." Doug stared out the window at the lavender twilight sky and the dark mountains carved with silver slopes. Up behind a copse of trees, the headlights of a Sno-Cat gleamed, the machine packing down powder for tomorrow's skiers.

Brooklyn Raine was Lyn Hill. Inn proprietor and driving force behind Ski-Hab. The Spidey-sense that had tingled all day intensified to an electric jolt.

"Tell me about Brooklyn Raine or Lyn Hill, or whatever she calls herself these days. Why does everyone protect her? And how did she get involved in Ski-Hab?"

"The reason everyone around here protects her is because Lyn wants to permanently put her celebrity behind her. She hasn't been in the spotlight in years. She despises the press and won't talk to any reporters."

The thought erupted from Doug's lips before his brain fully considered it. "I bet she'd talk to me."

Ace leaned forward, slamming his empty beer bottle on the coffee table. "Dude. Are you listening to me? If Lyn finds out you're a reporter, she'll not only refuse to talk to you, she'll bounce you out of Ski-Hab so fast, your butt will look like raw burger meat."

He brushed off the threat easily. The man who'd finagled interviews with imprisoned boxers, 'roid-raging wrestlers, and quarterbacks who'd just lost the Super Bowl would never be intimidated by an innkeeper. Even an innkeeper who'd dared to knock him to the ground.

"Okay." Doug kept his tone deceptively banal. "But if Brooklyn doesn't know about my trip to Iraq, how does she think I was injured?"

Ace shook his head. "I don't think she has any idea. Richie Armstrong, the acting director, said he would keep the deets as simple as possible. You're a civilian. You were wounded in an accident, and you were referred here by me."

He digested this information carefully, allowed his brain to play with different scenarios. Oh yeah. He could definitely parlay this situation into a public-interest piece. "Who knows the truth about how I came to be here?"

"You, me, and Richie Armstrong."

"That's it?" Doug pressed. "No one else?"

Ace's brow furrowed. "Like who?"

"Like Kerri-Sue?"

"Nope." Ace paused, rubbed the scruff on his chin, and then shook his head again, this time with more force. "No way. You think she would have walked away from your run-in with Lyn today if she knew? I'll bet Kerri-Sue did a little secret freak when Lyn cornered you two. You have to understand. Lyn stays in the background, like a shadow. She doesn't usually get involved for fear of recognition."

"So why'd she step in today with me?"

"Beats me." As if to emphasize his confusion, Ace shrugged halfheartedly.

"All the more reason why I need to talk to her again," Doug replied. "All day long, I've been thinking there's a great story here. And you just helped me find it."

"Whoa." Ace held up a hand. "You said you weren't interested in doing a story here because it had already been done."

"The story of *Ski-Hab* was already done." For the first time in months, Doug felt excitement tingle through his veins. No way would he give up this euphoria. Right arm or no right arm, he was a reporter. And in Brooklyn Raine, he sensed the story that could reignite his career.

"There hasn't been any information about Brooklyn Raine in nearly ten years," he said aloud, while his brain continued to play with the whys and wherefores. "Where she's been, what she's done, and her involvement in the Ski-Hab program. People would love to know this stuff. Throw in the stories of the soldiers she's helped, and it's a gold mine of human interest."

His comeback article. He might even include his own journey—a little behind-the-scenes with an actual participant of Ski-Hab. His editor would salivate when he found out.

"You're forgetting one thing," Ace said solemnly. "You're retired."

"Maybe I am." Doug drummed his fingers against his empty beer bottle. "Then again, maybe I'm not."

"I told you, man. If Lyn finds out you're a reporter—"

"Yeah, I know. But she has no idea how I was injured, right? So I could be anyone: a farmer injured in a combine accident, the victim of a shark attack, or maybe I'm suffering from some bizarre flesh-eating disease."

Ace frowned. "In other words, you're gonna lie to her."

"*You* lied to her."

"A, no I didn't," Ace retorted. "What Richie chose to tell her about you is between the two of them. In the lodge this afternoon, she asked how I knew you. I told her you helped me out of that jam at JFK. That was it. She didn't ask for anything more, and I didn't elaborate."

Doug snorted. "Semantics. You didn't lie, per se. You just omitted most of the truth."

"And B," Ace continued, pointedly ignoring Doug's comment, "I haven't established a reputation as a journalist with pristine ethics, like someone else in this room."

"Come off it, Ace. Because of my 'pristine ethics,' I'm not gonna do a hatchet job on the poor woman. I promise. She'll be extremely happy with the publicity she gets. I'll write her up as the Mother Theresa of the ski world. I won't even mention how she shoved me to the ground to prove a point."

"Wow." Sarcasm dripped like acid from the single word. "You really don't get it. To Lyn, *no* publicity is good publicity. She's got a real phobia about being recognized."

"Gimme a break. She practically grew up in the spotlight. She and Cheviot got engaged at Disney World, for God's sake, complete with a starring role in the Electric Parade. Now all of a sudden, she wants anonymity?"

"It's not 'all of a sudden.' She's been hiding from the world ever since her husband died."

"Too bad. The price of fame and fortune is having to live in the spotlight, whether you want to or not."

Ace shook his head. "Leave me out of this, dude. You wanna sell your soul for a story—"

"No." Sell his soul? Hardly. He was trying to regain his passion. Why couldn't Ace see that? "You don't get it."

"You got *that* right. And what's more, I don't want to. I don't want any part of this."

"Ace . . ." Doug inhaled deeply. "I *need* this story. For the first time in months, I'm jonesing to write. I'm even willing to use this"—he hefted his prosthetic arm—"if I have to. Or I'll check out that voice-activated software my orthopedist has been touting. This story could completely renew my life!"

"Yeah," Ace said blandly as he rose from the couch. "And destroy someone else's life in the process. Sorry, Doug. But I'm outta here."

Seconds later, the door to Doug's condo opened, then closed again on Ace's exit.

Chapter Six

After a fabulous dinner of pot roast with red-skinned potatoes and fingerling carrots, Lyn sat with Jeff and April in the parlor. Pine infused the air from the fresh boughs decorating the fireplace mantel. On the sideboard, assorted flavored brandies and liqueurs replaced the hot cider from the afternoon. Vivaldi's "Winter," a perennial favorite, played softly in the background through wall-mounted speakers.

The kids—exhausted, well-fed, and completely recovered from the afternoon's excitement—had shuffled off to bed a few minutes before.

Although Jeff and April included Lyn in their conversations, from anecdotes about the kids to wedding plans, she barely listened. Her mind remained fixed on the civilian from this afternoon, Mr. Sawyer.

When he'd risen the second time, after she'd pushed him, rage pulsated off him in waves hotter than the fire blazing in the hearth here. But then he'd paused and somehow pulled himself together. Good thing. Based on his size, if he'd given in to his first reaction, she'd probably be in the hospital right now. And she'd definitely deserve it.

Why *had* she pushed him, anyway? To do so was not only counterproductive but cruel as well. Ski-Hab's goal was to build its students *up,* not to knock them down. She should know. She wrote the mission statement when they'd incorporated the program.

A flush of shame warmed her cheeks. Since Ski-Hab's inception, she'd reviewed the students from that particular peak on the Snow Wonder trail hundreds of times. And in all those years, she'd seen dozens of participants falter when they fell. None had ever compelled her to any drastic action. Until Mr. Sawyer.

Poor Kerri-Sue, no doubt sensing something seriously wrong with Lyn's mental capacities, had immediately jumped to her charge's defense—which was absolutely the right reaction. And honestly, Mr. Sawyer had done nothing to deserve Lyn's heartless interference.

No. The one villain in today's event was Lyn herself. The idea stuck in her chest like an ice pick that stabbed her heart. Worse, a deep, knotting fear tied up her insides and nearly paralyzed her.

After Marc's death, she'd kept her emotions wrapped in a numbing cocoon. Now, all of a sudden, feelings she'd long ago suffocated had revived. She considered her envy of April's happiness, the attraction she'd sensed blooming between Becky and Ace Riordan, and, of course, her overreaction to Mr. Sawyer.

So the green monster had popped up when she saw how happy April was with Jeff and how obviously Jeff adored April. Of course Lyn would feel a pang of jealousy—the sharp reminder of what she and Marc had shared all too briefly.

And the episode with Ace and Becky? Merely a protective aunt guarding her niece's innocent heart from a possible tragedy, her saner self proclaimed.

But she had no easy explanation for what had happened today on Snow Wonder. Perhaps she should go back to that trail tomorrow, find Mr. Sawyer, and offer him an apology.

"You think Summer will go for it, Lyn?" April's question broke through her musings.

She shook herself back into the conversation. "Huh?"

"Help me plan the wedding," April replied with a blinding smile directed toward Jeff.

Had she missed something?

"You're going to ask *Summer* to help you?" When had the devil donned his ice skates? As long as she'd known them, for more than thirty years now, Summer and April had *never* gotten along.

"Well . . . yeah. You remember her wedding, don't you?" Once again, April swerved to face Jeff. "Everything perfect. Perfect spring day with the perfect blue sky, perfect gown, perfect bridesmaids' dresses. When she and Brad stepped out of the little stone church, a dozen white doves were released to take flight in a perfect arc. At the same time, white rose petals floated down from the top of the church. All in perfect precision."

Talk about a one-eighty. At the actual event, April had called this perfect precision, "Summer's Splendiferous Spousal Spectacular."

And *not* in a good way.

"So wait," Lyn said. "You want Summer to give you the same kind of thing? Rose petals and doves?"

"God, no." April shivered as if in the throes of some bizarre seizure, eyes bugged out and tongue lolling. "Could you just see me swathed in a thousand yards of white tulle while a cadre of birds flew around my face? I'd look like Cinderella on crack."

Lyn's delicate snickers were drowned out by Jeff's more thunderous laughter. Her older sister's self-deprecating humor apparently appealed to a wide audience.

"Let's face it," April added when the room quieted again, "Summer's much more organized than I am. And since the whole world is gonna be watching, I need as close to perfection as I can get. Without Summer to run her usual drill sergeant interference, I'll just make a muck of it."

Jeff picked up his fiancée's hand, clasped within his, and brushed a light kiss across her knuckles. "You can do this just fine on your own. I don't care what the rest of the world thinks. A nice, small intimate gathering is perfect enough for us. We're not exactly shooting for the cover of *People* magazine."

Understanding lit fireworks inside Lyn's brain. "Wait a minute. You're looking for perfection on your *wedding day* so you won't disappoint *the press?*"

"Yes." April rolled her eyes with all the subtle meaning of an angsty teenager. "I know. You think it's stupid—"

"No," Lyn interjected. "I understand. Honestly. I do. I've been there. Remember? From our first date in Oslo to the wedding at St. Patrick's Cathedral and the reception at the Waldorf?" And the honeymoon in St. Moritz, the years on the circuit as "the ski world's love bunnies." Followed a few short years later with the multiple trips to Memorial Sloan-Kettering's oncology center, all while cameras watched and recorded every single, agonizing moment. Right up to the funeral home and that vile photo of Marc's cancer-ravaged face lying on a white satin pillow in a gleaming cherrywood casket.

Pop! Inside the fireplace, a particularly dry piece of wood crackled and snapped beneath the roaring flames.

On a shiver, she pushed the ugly memories away.

Never again. Never again would she allow anyone to entertain the world with her pain. Or her joy. Or even her favorite color.

"Lyn?" Once again, April's voice brought her back from her solemn thoughts. "Are you okay?"

She forced a smile. "I'm fine. Just tired."

April immediately became contrite. "I'm sorry. We're keeping you awake, aren't we? I forgot how early you get up in the morning."

"It's all right," she said with a sigh. "Listen, April, Jeff? Can I give you one piece of advice?"

The couple exchanged a wary glance, then April nodded. "Sure."

"I know this may sound silly, but indulge me anyway. Try to think of the media as a giant monster with an unlimited appetite. You keep feeding it with photo ops and interviews and the monster keeps growing bigger and bigger. The bigger it grows, the hungrier it becomes. Until soon, you don't have enough to feed the media monster. And that's when it rips your heart out of your chest."

By secretly crashing a wake to take photos of your dead husband lying in his casket, which wind up splashed on the front page of every rag in the country.

"Don't do it, guys," she murmured. "Don't feed the monster. Please."

Ace would have probably been disappointed to know his departure came as a blessing to Doug. With the familiar adrenaline pumping through his blood, Doug called his editor in New York to talk about Ski-Hab, Brooklyn Raine, and his recent run-in with the former ski champ.

Jake practically salivated at the idea of a full-length feature article regarding the program and, more importantly, its heretofore unknown sponsor.

"You're sure it's her?" Jake's rapid speech communicated his eagerness to believe what Doug told him. "Brooklyn Raine. *The* Brooklyn Raine."

"The one and only," Doug said. "Ace confirmed it for me a few minutes ago. I'm guessing that's how he got to use the program for his community service. Apparently, he and Brooklyn know each other fairly well."

"You think they're an item?"

An image popped, unbidden, into Doug's head. Ace scanning the girls in the lodge with his biggest yes-I'm-who-you-think-I-am grin lighting up his beach boy features. Then the Coyote, eyes glittering with feral challenge. Brooklyn Raine and Ace Riordan? An item?

"No." No way the Coyote on the hill would come second to anyone in life. Not even Ace Riordan, snowboarding's Aerial Snowball. "Not a chance," he added for emphasis.

"Too bad."

"Excuse me?" Jake, looking for gossip? Since when?

"Women love a good romance, Doug. Particularly between a younger man and older woman. Cougars, they're calling 'em nowadays. By adding the female point of view, we could double our readership with a story like that. Remember Brooklyn's husband? Handsome guy struck down in his prime?"

"Marc Cheviot," he rattled off automatically.

"That's him. You remember when he died?"

"Vaguely." He'd been an intern at a small newspaper in Iowa at the time, in charge of digging up the research on Cheviot's accomplishments on the slopes for the obituary. Hadn't really thought about Marc Cheviot since. Until now.

"Every reporter worth his ink had a piece of that press pie," Jake was saying. "The world wept. It was beautiful. One of those perfect news stories that touched *everyone*. Men, women, kids, Americans, Canadians, Europeans, sports fans, romance fans, gossip fans. For a full week, the global spotlight shone on Cheviot and his widow. Then, after it was all over, the widow disappeared." Jake paused to take a breath, but before Doug could say anything, he pressed on. "You're sure it's her? Ace confirmed it? How? When? Give me particulars, Sawyer."

Doug offered a quick rundown, skipping over his many conversations with Ace regarding his adolescent crush.

"So Ace never let on until now," Jake replied. "That alone tells me there's a story in this somewhere. Something sweet and juicy. My eye's twitching like a jackhammer."

Jake considered his facial tic akin to a personal Magic 8 Ball. The more his eyelid fluttered, the hotter the story promised to be. Like Doug, Jake sensed a bombshell in Ski-Hab. Unlike Doug, Jake wouldn't be interested in the heartwarming aspect, but in the secrecy.

"You've got a former ski champion dumping money into a program to help disabled vets. And she isn't looking for publicity? Why? What's she got to hide?"

"Probably nothing—"

"Cow pods. All women have something to hide, Sawyer. Remember that. You'll save yourself a lot of heartache."

"Right," Doug replied, biting back most of the sarcasm that tingled on his tongue. "What was I thinking?"

According to legend, Jake's chauvinistic attitude had first flared when women reporters were finally allowed in men's locker rooms a few decades ago. His animosity had only increased in volatility with the appearance of the WNBA, Danica Patrick in the Indy, and Muhammad Ali's daughter in the boxing ring.

Of course, his four marriages and consecutive divorces only added to his suspicions regarding ulterior motives in the fairer sex.

"What do you need from me?" Jake asked.

This time, Doug didn't hesitate. "A laptop with voice-activated typing software and a steady source of Internet service. Wi-Fi is spotty up in the mountains."

"I'll have it expressed to you first thing tomorrow. And Doug?"

"Yeah?"

"Welcome back."

For the first time in months, sheer joy warmed Doug from the inside out. "Thanks."

Chapter Seven

At precisely 3:45 the next afternoon, Lyn stood on the same crest between Snow Blind and Snow Wonder. A paper-white sky surrounded her, and the air held that sharp clean scent of coming snow.

Once again, she studied the group of students, this time, though, paying special attention to the man working under Kerri-Sue's tutelage. He seemed more confident today, more in tune with his skis and his balance. The uncertainty she'd sensed yesterday had evaporated like mist over the mountains.

Now, Kerri-Sue stood at the bottom of the hill, looking up at her protégé, much as Lyn stared down from above—twin guardian angels. Meanwhile, Mr. Sawyer carved perfect S-shaped lines, working the pole in his left hand with precision to propel him downhill at a steady, even pace. His skis dug deep grooves into the packed powder, his knees clearly pushing with all their might. How quickly he'd become acclimated to the balance needed with one arm! Almost as if some inner demon drove him to succeed.

As Lyn watched, an idea glimmered in her brain. She knew exactly what she had to do. Before logic or fear could take hold and dissuade her, she barreled down from the top of the hill until she skied beside him.

His double take registered surprise at her approach, and he came to a hard stop with a *scritch* of his skis on the hard-packed snow. When she halted alongside him, frown lines etched the area around his full lips. He lifted his arm, and his ski pole flew, nearly hitting her shoulder. Luckily, she leaned back, out of harm's reach.

Without so much as an apology, he gripped the edge of his goggles and yanked them atop his gleaming black helmet. Cock-eyed, of course. Some one-handed skills still eluded him. His eyes, a clear hazel that reflected gray, green, and gold, glittered feral in his sharp, angular face.

My God. He's the Big Bad Wolf. And I'm about to tangle with him? After yesterday?

Anxiety skittered like ball bearings over her nerve endings. She sucked in icy air, felt the old Brooklyn Raine persona rouse inside her.

Breathe deeply. Maybe he doesn't remember you.

"What'd I do wrong this time, Ms. Hill?"

Dagnabbit. He remembered her.

She gulped a huge ball of emotion, a jumble of exhilaration and dread she hadn't experienced since her competition days.

He was older than she'd originally thought, probably close to her own age. A refreshing change from the twentysomethings normally involved in Ski-Hab. And not bad looking, if only he wouldn't scowl at her so lethally.

Down, girl. Lyn silently scolded the inner Brooklyn. Unfortunately, once awakened, the old Brooklyn didn't surrender easily.

Oh, come on, Lyn. Look at him! She studied Mr. Sawyer with the smoldering awareness of a female alone too long. *Hubba, hubba.*

"Well?" he demanded. "Go ahead already. List my errors and faults. Just be sure to keep your hands to yourself this time. What would you like to correct for me today?"

She could have taken offense, could have responded with her own biting retort. Instead, she offered a weak smile. "Nothing. In fact, as far as I know, you did nothing wrong yesterday either. And yet, you've improved vastly since I was unforgivably rude to you."

"I—" He started to say something, but she cut him off with a quick upraised hand.

She didn't dare allow him to argue. Given half an opportunity to hesitate, she'd back down for sure.

"No, please. Let me finish." To make sure he heeded her

request, she rushed through the rest of what she planned to say. "I've been watching you a good part of today."

God, that didn't sound right at all. Made her seem like some crazed stalker. He must have thought so too because one sooty eyebrow arched in her direction.

Somewhere deep inside her brain, Brooklyn Raine gripped the helm. Taking advantage of Lyn's hesitancy, she careened to the front of the personality line.

Oh, for heaven's sake, could you screw this up any worse?

Well, let's find out, shall we?

Watch and learn, honey.

"I'm not a stalker or anything. Honest. I was hoping to come up with a way to atone for my behavior yesterday. What I did . . . pushing you like that? It was horrible. I mean, I think back on it, replaying it in my mind, you know? And I can't believe I did such a vicious, cruel thing."

"Yeah, well, that makes two of us," he said.

Strangely, she detected more humor than malice in his tone. And the lines around his mouth—his generous, full mouth— smoothed. At least he hadn't hauled off and slugged her. Yet.

On a deep breath, she plowed on. "I'm really very sorry. And I'd like to make it up to you."

"Lyn?" Kerri-Sue's iron-laced question came from behind her.

She whirled. And frowned. Apparently, Kerri-Sue had called in the cavalry. Because there was Richie Armstrong on Kerri-Sue's left and Ace Riordan on her right. They flanked her, a wall of disapproval with folded arms and tight lips drawn into stern lines.

Lyn returned Kerri-Sue's frigid glare.

Tattletale.

As if she gained strength from the men behind her, Kerri-Sue snorted. With her eyebrows arched, she added, "Can we help you with something today?"

Oh, for heaven's sake. She wasn't some ax murderer who'd targeted Mr. Sawyer as her next victim.

"No." She layered her voice with enough ice to freeze Miami Beach. "I was simply speaking to Mr. Sawyer."

"Since that went so well yesterday?" Kerri-Sue retorted.
Wow. The hostility radiating around the trio momentarily
left Lyn speechless.
"Mr. Sawyer." Kerri-Sue faced him, her posture ramrod stiff.
"Let me apologize for Ms. Hill's repeated attempts to accost
you. I have no idea why she's here again today, but we won't
allow a repeat of yesterday."
"Actually"—Mr. Sawyer looked over the wall of outrage, then
winked at Lyn. *Winked* at her!—"Ms. Hill was doing a fairly
decent job of apologizing on her own before you interrupted us."
Kerri-Sue visibly started. "She was?"
"Yes, I was." Amazing how she managed to strike the right
tone between nonchalant and amused. Inside, Lyn simmered.
If Kerri-Sue weren't one of the best instructors in Ski-Hab
history, she'd be unemployed right now. Only her stellar results and Lyn's own reticence to announce her link to the program in front of a stranger saved Kerri-Sue from a speedy
termination announcement. By the end of the day, though, she
and Richie would be having a looooooong talk about Kerri-
Sue's future with the organization. Right now, however, Lyn
intended to communicate her displeasure in another manner.
Give the pretty instructor fair warning of what was to come,
in her own subtle way.
"As a matter of fact," Lyn stated flatly, "I was so impressed
with his improvement since yesterday, I was about to ask him
to join me on a bigger slope for the final run of the day."
Hard to tell who was more flabbergasted by that announcement: Mr. Sawyer, Kerri-Sue, or Lyn herself. Even Richie looked
slack-jawed and bug-eyed all of a sudden.
Okay. So originally, she'd only intended to invite him for a
cup of coffee after today's lesson. Too bad Kerri-Sue's snide
insinuations had pushed her into challenge territory.
Lyn Hill wouldn't be suckered in by a dare from anyone.
She was a mature woman, a widow. But rile the old Brooklyn
Raine, and she'd never back down. As different from Lyn Hill
as a ski parka was from a bikini.
In the past, she'd never had trouble separating those two
individuals and their unique personalities. Until today. Or

maybe yesterday. Brooklyn, after all, would definitely push a struggling man to the ground in a fit of impatience, while Lyn wouldn't dream of placing her hands on another person. Certainly not in exasperation or violence or pique or whatever had been going through her mind at the time.

Still . . .

The final run of the day had always belonged to her and Marc. Together. Alone. From the day they first arrived at Mount Elsie, each late afternoon, immediately after they hit the chairs, operators would close down the lift to all other riders.

Following Marc's death, Lyn had continued the tradition. Alone. Always alone. Friends, family, Mount Elsie's staff—they all knew how she valued that last opportunity for peace at the end of every ski day. She used the time to commune with nature, with Marc's spirit, and with her bittersweet memories.

Why on earth had she just invited this stranger along? To join her for the one part of her day she'd always reserved for herself alone? Worse, why did she *crave* his agreement to her invitation?

"Lyn?" Kerri-Sue's question drifted into her musings. "Are you sure?"

Well, well. There was one good thing. Her sudden announcement had converted Kerri-Sue from antagonist to gal-pal. Didn't that just warm the cockles of her heart?

Good thing too. Lyn hated firing people.

"I'm sure," she said with a firm nod.

The wind whistled the high-pitched song of a pending snow squall. Ace looked like she'd just announced she was really a three-footed alien. Richie simply shook his head, perhaps wondering if he should have his hearing checked. Maybe she should go with him. Have her head examined.

Didn't matter. With or without her inner Brooklyn in control, no way Lyn would back down now. Not with all these eyes staring at her.

To her surprise, though, Ace's glare swerved toward Mr. Sawyer. "I'm not so sure that's a good idea."

"Sure it is," Mr. Sawyer exclaimed. A broad smile lit up his face.

Once again, a pang of loneliness struck Lyn's heart. When was the last time a man—a good-looking man, at that—seemed so eager to spend time with her?

"I'm more than ready to ski with Ms. Hill," Mr. Sawyer added.

Warmth tingled through Lyn's veins.

"No, you're not," Ace replied, with way too much force to Lyn's mind.

"I won't take a diamond run," she assured Ace. "We'll hit Snow Business."

A mid-mountain run with a blue square trail for intermediate skiers. Lyn always considered green dot trails, meant for beginners, too flat for anyone to have fun. Terrain without a lot of hills translated to a skier expending tons of energy just to keep forward and downhill momentum. All that struggle often led to frustration and, sometimes, injuries. Not the best way to get a newbie to fall in love with a sport.

"No." Ace practically bit the word over his teeth. "Besides, Doug and I have plans."

"We do?" Mr. Sawyer sounded genuinely surprised.

Welcome to the club, pal. There's a lot of that going around.

She stole a quick glance in his direction, caught doubt clouding his features.

Ace laughed. "Dude, those painkillers are seriously messing with your brain."

An undercurrent of tension flickered between Ace and Mr. Sawyer. Subtle, but Lyn felt it. Could practically taste the unease in the frosty air. Something was definitely going on between these two. Something bizarre and not quite as jovial as they both tried to play.

Meanwhile, Richie and Kerri-Sue directed their own radioactive charges at Lyn. Small wonder the tree line didn't spontaneously combust with all the heat in their circle of friends.

"Shouldn't you be spending this time with your niece and nephew, Lyn?" Richie asked pointedly.

Lyn guessed what he really meant was, *Have you lost your mind?*

The expected answer? *Of course not.* The inevitable answer? *Maybe.*

Rather than allow Richie into her private turmoil, she tossed her head. "Becky and Michael are with their mother and soon-to-be stepfather. Doing a little family bonding in Lake Champlain today. Really, Richie, it's not that big a deal. One run with Mr. Sawyer. I promise I'll take good care of him. It's not like I don't know how."

Now, see? Here was the problem with Brooklyn Raine. Let her out of her cage for a minute, and she commandeered the spotlight. Worse, now that she had an audience waiting for her to admit she'd made a mistake, Brooklyn would never budge. Throw in the fact that this was the first guy to raise her awareness quotient in aeons, and they'd have better luck stopping an avalanche.

"What do you say, Mr. Sawyer?" she pressed. "Would you like to join me?"

Chapter Eight

Doug could barely contain his delight. Talk about the mountain coming to Mohammed! He'd spent half the night trying to concoct a reasonable scenario that would allow him to casually bump into Lyn Hill, aka Brooklyn Raine, again. The best he'd been able to dream up was to get off the bunny hill as quickly as possible and hope for a chance encounter.

With a plan in mind, however lame, he buried his self-pity and faced today's lessons with Kerri-Sue the way a condemned man might view a last-minute reprieve from the governor. One last chance to fix his life and move on. Or give up for good.

To his surprise, the old skills from all those lessons in West Virginia had come back. Of course, the equipment had vastly improved over the last two decades. Today, Doug had seized his moment. And look how quickly fate had rewarded him.

"I'd love to join you."

Careful, he warned himself. Don't look too eager.

"*If,*" he added, "you think I'm ready."

"I've already told you, Doug." Ace managed to eke through his disapproving frown. "You're not."

"Come on, Ace," Lyn interjected. "It's Snow Business—a dozen hills, and a nice, even incline. No moguls or steep drops. Only difference between this slope and that one is that Snow Business is longer."

"It has nothing to do with the difficulty of the slope," Ace replied.

"Oh?" Her hands shot to her hips—a confrontational pose Doug would bet his left arm Ace had never before seen from a woman. "So what's the problem?"

Ace leveled a cool stare at Doug. "Ask *him.*"

Lyn's focus veered to him, and she frowned. "Mr. Sawyer? What am I missing here?"

"I have absolutely no idea." He offered her a shrug and a quirky smile. "I didn't even know Ace was tracking my progress so closely. Tell you what, though. Why don't we let Kerri-Sue be the judge? She's been working with me out here on the slopes and inside in the gym. She knows what I can and can't do by now."

"That's not what I meant and you know it," Ace snapped.

"Umm . . ." Kerri-Sue held up her gloved hands. "I'm not sure . . ."

Scanning the group around him, Doug realized he was the only one enjoying this debacle. Everyone else, including Brooklyn or Lyn or whoever, wore a fierce look of either dread or umbrage. What was going on? This wasn't exactly life and death stuff. He'd seen happier expressions in foxholes.

Had he ever fretted over the trivial like this? Funny how perspectives changed when daily living meant dodging incendiary devices, fending off sniper fire, and, of course, dealing with a missing limb.

He cast a glance at the soldiers on the sideline. They would understand his confusion. They knew all about living in the moment. And PTSD, and the loss of friends, and returning to a home where they weren't always welcome.

"This is ridiculous," Brooklyn said at last. "Look, I'm heading over to the triple chairlift. If Mr. Sawyer decides to join me, that would be wonderful. If not, I'll take the run alone. End of story."

In a repeat performance from yesterday, she pushed off with her poles and *shussed* away.

Oh no, you don't. You're not getting away easy this time.

With a quick salute to the cluster of frowning individuals, Doug flashed a grin at Ace. "See ya." He fumbled with his goggles on his helmet but managed to slide them into place, shove off on his one pole, and propel himself forward. "Hey, Ms. Hill, wait up."

To his surprise, she stopped. And waited for him to catch

up. The smile on her face reminded him of all those toothpaste ads she'd done in the nineties. God, she still had it: that sparkle he remembered from years ago. Whereas in her youth she'd packaged her wow factor in a sassy look and confident manner, this woman drew his attention thanks to her wistful quality, a hint of sadness that tinged her eyes.

He felt his conscience being zapped, an electric pulse of guilt, but he mentally shoved away the sensation. Brooklyn Raine's smile, sad or otherwise, represented his way back. After surviving the stormiest episode of his life and landing broken on the rocks, she had become his beacon, his rainbow—the promise of better days to come.

"Thanks for coming along," she said.

"Thanks for inviting me."

Once he neared her, she pointed one ski pole at a small break in the otherwise heavy tree line. "Go up this way and down the other side," she directed. "And don't stop or you'll never maintain the speed necessary to make it to the lift from here."

He skied into the pine and birch-framed path, then caught the downward slope and picked up speed. The narrow route gave him just enough of an incline to allow his skis to glide onward. Snow-covered needles brushed his jacket in soft whiffs.

Seconds later, he wended his way into the clearing that brought him to the end of a longer trail, a few feet from the boarding area for the triple chairlift. A chairlift that had already stopped running for the day.

A lanky teenage boy rearranged the gates to block anyone from entering. Near the steps leading to the lodge, the diehard snow enthusiasts popped off their skis before trudging inside to pack up gear or regroup in the upstairs tavern for some après-ski fun.

Doug blew out a breath of frustration. Too late. He'd missed his opportunity by mere seconds.

"Keep going!" Brooklyn shouted from behind him. "Don't stop now."

He pushed himself forward, but she sped past him in a blur of black and red. Skis spitting snow, she stopped near the kid at the gates while Doug inched slowly toward the quiet lift.

Whatever she said, Doug couldn't hear, but the boy nodded and stepped aside to pull the barriers apart.

"Come on." Brooklyn waved Doug closer.

He barely edged inside the black vinyl tape before the teen closed off the entrance once again.

"Give me two seconds," the kid said as he ran to the booth beside the boarding area. "I'll let Ryan know you're on your way up." Once inside the booth, he picked up the phone.

On a squeal and hum of machinery, the chairs began ascending again.

Brooklyn Raine broke into a little hip shimmy reminiscent of her ski style so many years ago. "Shall we, Mr. Sawyer?"

"Doug," he corrected, and faced the front of the boarding area.

Inside the booth, the teen hung up the receiver and flashed a thumbs-up.

Clumping forward on his skis, Doug asked the woman beside him, "How'd you do that?"

"Do what?" For a moment, she looked genuinely puzzled by the question. Her finely arched brows peaked, and her eyes crinkled in the late afternoon sun. "Oh, you mean the lift?" She shrugged. "I know people."

"Yeah," he murmured, biting back a smile. "I bet you do."

One of the chairs in the line made the turn, and Lyn deftly maneuvered to the right side for Mr. Sawyer's benefit. She pushed forward with him now on her left, allowing him the use of his one arm to board the next triple chair as easily as possible. When she craned her neck, she caught a glimpse of her companion's profile. Despite the helmet with the goggles once again askew on top—a look that would make even Arnold Schwarzenegger seem like a helpless wuss—Mr. Sawyer gave the impression of a man of great strength. Probably in personality as well as in physical stature.

Those gorgeous hazel eyes she'd seen flash in anger and amusement sat perfectly above razor-sharp cheekbones and a well-defined jaw. He towered over her, maybe stood as tall as six and a half feet, and even with the padding of his ski jacket and pants, she discerned a broad upper body, tapering to slimmer hips. All in all, she sensed a man accustomed to going after life with both hands.

How would such a man react to the sudden loss of a crucial limb?

Not well, she figured. After all, how would *she* react if she were in his boots? That old photo of the H-bomb's dust cloud over Hiroshima filled her imagination. Yeah. Something like that.

The chairback hit her knees, and she collapsed into the hard, cold seat as Mr. Sawyer did the same. When they were settled, she raised her hand to lower the overhead bar. He couldn't help—not if he wanted to keep his grip on his ski pole, but he made the gesture anyway.

"I've got it," she assured him.

He lowered his hand, and she pulled the rail to slowly sink the bar into place. *Clunk!*

She set her skis on the footrest, and he followed suit. Silence reigned, broken only by the *whoosh* of a snow gun on some trail beyond the tree line, and the creaky sound of the chairlift as the overhead cables wound through the flywheels.

The overwhelming heat of self-consciousness flared in Lyn's cheeks, then steamed up her hairline. God, she was an idiot. No good at small talk, never had been. But she had to say *something* to the man.

"Umm . . ."

Oh, excellent start. This whole sorry episode kept getting better and better.

When she turned to face him, he smiled. "Am I making you nervous?"

Someone shoot me. Shoot me now. "I . . . umm . . . I don't usually invite strangers to ski with me."

He didn't laugh at her. Score one point in the sensitivity column. In fact, his expression reflected genuine concern. "Should I be flattered?"

Despite her nervousness, a giggle escaped. "Take it any way you like. But honestly? I'm terrified."

"Of me?" His tone registered disbelief. "Why?"

"Because I don't know you. And since you don't know me, let me tell you. I don't do this."

"Do what? Share a chairlift with someone you don't know? Let me make it easier for you. My name's Doug. I live in New York. Oh, and in case you haven't noticed, I'm missing my right arm."

"Yeah, I got that." Tension eased from her neck and shoulders. "Can I ask . . . ?" She looked down at the trails below, the white swaths like satin ribbons in an expanse of spiky trees and lumpy gray rocks. "What happened to you?"

"Car accident . . . well, more like a Jeep accident. Me and a couple of buddies rolled over an embankment."

"I'm sorry. Were your friends all right?"

"Died on impact, I was told. I don't really know what happened. I woke up in a hospital with no arm and no memory beyond getting into the ride at the start of the day."

"They say that's for the best," she replied.

"Do they?" He arched a brow in her direction, but the easy grin never left his lips.

She relaxed even more and actually found her own smile. "Well, yes. Supposedly, it helps with the healing process and keeps you from dwelling on the injuries."

"And who exactly are 'they'?"

The lilt he placed on that last word communicated how he delighted in teasing her. All shreds of anxiety wafted away on the crisp air. "The medical professionals," she replied loftily. "Surgeons, physical therapists, even my . . . *the* students here all say that not remembering the details is often a blessing."

"Ah."

She'd almost lost control with her slip about her students. Better to turn the subject far away from this place before she made a major gaffe. "You said you live in New York?"

"Mmm-hmm. Manhattan. Upper East Side."

"Nice."

"Yeah, it was. Until my mother moved in."

"Your mother?" She couldn't shield her surprise if she'd tried. The *last* description she would have used on this man was Mama's Boy.

He nodded and rolled his eyes more dramatically than her niece Becky on her best day. "Part of the trials of being the only child of a single parent. After I was discharged from the hospital and sent home, she moved into my apartment to take care of me."

A pang of regret struck Lyn's heart. "That's sweet." In the last decade, *her* mother had refused to visit, always insisting Lyn come to her. Even when Marc had passed away.

She and her mother had never been close. Of course, she'd spent six months—sometimes more—of the year with her father on the ski circuit. Mom, strong-willed, independent, and often abrasive, seemed content with an absentee husband for half the year. But was she really? Or had she just made the best of the situation her husband had presented her? And did she still resent her youngest daughter for causing a rift in their marriage?

"She would have come on this trip if I hadn't brought Ace instead."

Lyn blinked. For a moment, she'd fallen into memories better left unexplored. But Mr. Sawyer's statement came at the right time to jolt her back to the present.

"Ace," she said thoughtfully. Now there was a conundrum. "You do know he's got a competition in Canada, right?"

"I know. He's not staying much longer. He'll train as much as he can here—"

"Here? At Mount Elsie?" Despite her best efforts, amusement escaped with a snort. "With its twelve-hundred-foot vertical?"

Mr. Sawyer nodded. "I know. In competition terms, this is like snowboarding down a residential driveway. Which is why I've insisted he leave by the end of the week. He's got access to a private course a few hundred miles from here. They're building up the terrain park to challenge him and get him completely ready for next month's games."

She shot an inquisitive stare his way. "And you know all this because . . . ?"

"He told me."

Puh-leez. "And you believe him?"

"Ace would never lie to me." For the first time since they'd sat on the lift, he frowned. "He knows better."

"What exactly is your relationship to him anyway?"

Chapter Nine

Doug stared at the approaching tower, almost willing the chairlift to pick up speed. Good Lord, how many lies would he have to tell in a ten-minute trip? He'd already skirted around how he'd lost his arm.

Bitterness burned his throat. His roundabout tale minimized the loss of hero Giles Markham and five other brave men to "a couple of buddies." Not only that, he managed to make the tragedy of war sound like a bunch of drunks who'd lost control during a joyride. Wow, there was something to be proud of.

All the more reason, perhaps, why he had to tell this story to readers of *The Sportsman*. Odd how the more time he spent with Brooklyn Raine, the more he burned to return to his keyboard.

"Ace said you helped him when he got into trouble at JFK two years ago," Brooklyn prompted. "Are you a lawyer?"

"No." *Okay, deep breath.* So far, he'd only omitted the full truth, not totally reconstructed it. Could he continue to slip and slide around the facts? Lying didn't come easily to him. Never had. His tongue felt thick, and his lungs sputtered for air.

"So?" She arched her brows. "What's your story?"

Ha. And Ace thought she feared reporters? Why would she? In fact, she'd make a great reporter herself. She had just as much tenacity when it came to a subject that caught her attention.

"I've known Ace since his first competition days." When the then-thirteen-year-old lit the X-Games on fire with his signature big air trick, the Bump and Grind. In the first of many articles Doug would write about Ace Riordan, he'd forecasted the kid's meteoric rise to the top of the snowboarding world after that one amazing aerial flip.

"So," Brooklyn said, "you're like his agent or something?" He hesitated. "I'm . . . more like . . . promotion." Oh, he was skating on very thin ice right now.

Understanding widened her eyes. Since she was a former ski champion, she must have recalled her own glory days and the entourage of legal, promotional, and athletic personnel swamping her every move. Easy enough, based on the information he'd provided, for her to assume he was just another face in a sports superstar's crowd.

"Of course," she replied with a wry smile. "I would imagine protecting Ace's image is a twenty-four/seven job."

"There've definitely been some scary moments in the past." Not much of a lie there. Ace was still a kid, dealing with the type of fame that sent more highly experienced adults spiraling into self-destruction. "But since my accident, I've been pretty much unemployed."

"Ace *fired* you?" Her eyes narrowed in outrage.

He bit back a smile. Well, well. The Coyote really did have a heart. Who knew? "No. Ace didn't fire me. Technically, I don't work for him."

"So your company fired you? That's just as bad."

"No. No one fired me. I just haven't been able to do my job since I left the hospital."

"Why on earth not?" Outrage transformed to confusion.

"You really need to ask?"

"Of course."

"Yoo-hoo." He flapped his empty sleeve with the intensity of a hawk swooping in on a disabled mouse. *Thwap, thwap, thwap.* "Does this little tragedy ring a bell for you?"

"Tragedy? Is that how you see your injury?"

"Don't." He held up his left hand, the ski pole punctuating the frosty air like an exclamation point. "Don't try to force-feed me any platitudes about challenges and life not giving me more than I can handle. I've heard them all, and I'm not buying any of them."

"Okay, so wait. Let me get this straight. You think because you're missing an arm you can't work anymore?"

"Yeah, I did."

Her narrowed eyes glinted steel in the surrounding twilight.

"*Can't?* Or *won't* work anymore?"

"Can't or won't. Doesn't matter."

"Wanna bet?"

On second thought, the Coyote must have had some barracuda DNA in her genetic makeup. "I said I *did* feel that way." And for the first time since he'd sat beside her on this lift, he gave her the full truth. "Until I met you."

She actually blushed, and offered a thousand-watt smile that made him feel sixteen again.

More time. He needed more time with this snow siren who both infuriated and charmed him. Oh sure, mainly for his article but also because—oh my God, she was *Brooklyn Raine.*

The love-struck teen he'd once been couldn't quite abandon his awe in his idol's presence. How many people got this kind of opportunity? Not many, he'd bet.

Now or never.

Doug seized his moment. "Would you have dinner with me tonight?"

His question hung between them unanswered. Not that Lyn hadn't heard him. In fact, she'd heard him all too clearly. At least, until the words pressed a blaring panic button inside her head.

Omigod, omigod, omigod. How on earth should she answer?

In a frantic attempt to find an escape, she noticed the sign mounted on the tower as they passed. PREPARE TO UNLOAD. RAISE BAR.

Thank God.

Feigning nonchalance, she gestured with a nod in that direction. "Put your goggles back into place, and take your skis off the footrest," she directed. "We're about to hit the ramp."

"You didn't answer my question."

He noticed. The bottom dropped out of her stomach, hurtling her heart into freefall. Her gloved hand tightened on the restraint bar as she looked away from his intense stare. "I—I can't."

"Can't or won't?" The teasing lilt returned to his tone.

Can't, won't. What was the difference? The mere idea of sitting across from this man over an intimate meal, where he could study her more intently, slipped an itchy sweater over her skin. She pushed the bar up and out of the way, then sidled to the edge of her seat—more from discomfort than in preparation to ski off the chair. "Do you need help getting off the lift?"

"Are you deliberately changing the subject?"

From the corner of her eye, she gauged the distance to the incline and the gear house. "My question needs an answer right away. Yours can wait."

"That's a matter of opinion."

Her attention swerved back to him pronto. "What is? Whether or not you need help getting off the lift? You may not believe this, but I'm pretty familiar with the Ski-Hab program, so you needn't feel embarr—"

"Will you have dinner with me?"

The ramp loomed closer. "Would you forget about that right now? Do you need help getting off the lift? Yes or no?"

"Answer my question first. Will you have dinner with me tonight? Yes or no?"

God, no. But she couldn't turn him down flat. Not after yesterday's fiasco. The last thing she wanted was to hurt the man's feelings. Again. Her skis hit the front of the ramp with a *thump-swish*. "Can we talk about this later? Please?"

He shrugged, leaning back, totally at odds with her ready-to-spring-from-the-lift stance. "I can continue to sit here and make the kid in the booth take me back down on the chair if you don't say yes," he threatened.

Well, wouldn't *that* tick off Ryan, the kid in the booth? And Kevin, in the other booth, who was probably waiting at the bottom end of the lift with one foot out the door? Kevin hadn't exactly been thrilled that she'd chosen his particular lift to ride after closing time. Apparently, the kid had some major video game competition at a friend's house tonight, and her request was going to make him sit out the first round. Now, if he had to wait for Mr. Sawyer to come back down to the base area? Annoyance pricked her nape. A ticked-off Kevin would complain to *everyone*, and she'd become the mountain's resident pariah.

The chair hovered near the end of the unloading zone. Her skis flattened against the crest. They had breaths of time now before the chair would swing around, and Ryan would either have to stop the lift for them to jump off or take them back down the other side, their last run of the day nothing more than a missed opportunity and a thorn in Kevin's side.

"Yes or no, Ms. Hill?" Mr. Sawyer pressed.

Three . . .

Ridiculous. Aside from guests at her bed-and-breakfast, she didn't dine with strangers. And certainly not dinner, which denoted a certain romantic connotation.

Two . . .

Besides, she had to go home. Had things to do. April, Jeff, and the kids might already be back from their day trip to Lake Champlain—particularly if they left, oh, say, fifteen minutes after they arrived there.

One . . .

Her arguments crumbled. "All right, all right! Yes. I'll go to dinner with you. Now get off!" She lifted her bottom off the seat, felt the chair push her down the opposite side of the ramp.

As she made the turn around the massive steel tower of the lift, the swish of his skis beside her broke the silence. Five seconds later, the hum of the chairlift ground to a halt. At least Kevin would only miss the first round. And maybe he wouldn't hold it against her forever.

Mr. Sawyer zipped closer and flashed a smug grin. "There now. Was that so hard?"

"No." She clenched her teeth to bite back the rest of her retort.

"But . . . ?" he prompted.

So much for keeping her thoughts to herself. The man was perceptive, she'd grant him that much. Somehow, he'd become fully aware she had more to say. Okay, fine. He wanted to know? She'd let him have it with both barrels. "Look, Mr. Sawyer—"

"Doug," he corrected.

"Doug," she said with a sigh. "The only reason you got me to agree was because you used blackmail."

"Blackmail?" His eyes rounded in mock innocence, sooty lashes batting surprise clearer than Morse code's SOS. "I never resort to blackmail. It was a *dare*."

A shiver rippled her spine. A dare. Why did he have to dare her?

She stopped at the crest of the first hill and inhaled the crisp, clean air for fortitude. When he halted beside her, she studied him cryptically. Something about Doug Sawyer put her on edge. Not in a bad way. More like the adrenaline rush she used to experience immediately before the buzzer sounded at the start of a competition. An addictive high she'd kicked years ago. Or at least, she'd *thought* she kicked it.

"Wanna race to the bottom?"

His question must have become mangled in her gray matter. He couldn't possibly have asked . . .

She blinked. Didn't he have any idea who he challenged? No, of course not. Why would he?

Despite the electricity tingling in her veins at the thought of a race, she shook her head. "I don't think so."

"Afraid I'll beat you, huh? Well, that's understandable. I'm a big threat. A one-armed recent graduate of the bunny slope who's got at least eighty pounds and about fourteen inches on you. Yes, sir. Which anyone who took basic physics courses can tell ya translates into a real speed demon on a downhill."

"That's precisely why I won't race you," she replied. "When I win, you'll be crushed."

"*When* you win?" He mimed an arrow piercing his chest, complete with the slight stagger backward and the exaggerated expression of pain. "Aw, now you've gone and wounded my male pride. Again."

"Again?"

He tilted his head toward hers. Dear God, his eyes would peer into her soul if she let them. To prevent such an occurrence, she veered her gaze to the trail below them. Not quite as smooth as she would have liked. Some icy patches, one or two sparse areas where brown grass peeked up through the veneer.

"You do recall when you planted me in the snow yesterday, right?" he said dryly.

Her focus snapped back to him, face filling with heat. "I told you I was sorry about that—" His laughter stopped her in mid-excuse. "You're teasing me?"

"No, I'm *challenging* you." He shoved the point of his pole into the snow. "For fun. And to challenge myself. I was a fairly decent skier before my accident. You've given me my first opportunity to really find out what I can do with this." He flapped his empty sleeve again. "Let's open 'er up and see what happens. What do you think?"

What did she think? A challenge. The air crackled, as if she'd pulled a woolen cap from her hair. She smiled. "What if I win?"

"If you win, I slink back to the bunny hill, honorably defeated. What's more, I release you from our dinner date."

Date? The smile evaporated, and she gulped the anxiety rising in her throat. A . . . *date?* He really was asking her on a date?

"And you can go back to"—he paused—"whatever it is you planned to do tonight."

Yeah, right. What she'd planned was basically what she always did on Tuesday nights. Dinner alone, followed by watching Mrs. Bascomb's stellar imitation of Madame Defarge for an hour or two. In bed by ten with the evening news and lights out before the weatherman predicted the next snowfall. Oh, sure. Rip-roarin' times at Snowed Inn Bed-and-Breakfast.

"But if I win," he continued, "we keep our date."

"Not a date. An engagement," she corrected, then practically bit her tongue in half. Good God, that sounded even worse than *date.*

And of course, his grin let her know he had no intention of allowing her to wriggle out of her own trap.

"Engagement?" He batted his eyes, cupped his left hand near his chin like a schoolgirl. "Gee, this is so sudden. Is it okay if I take some time to think about it? I mean, I like you and all, but—"

"Okay! Okay! You're on!" Anything to stop his inanity. Besides, the rush of icy wind from a good downhill sprint just might cool the burn in her cheeks before she spontaneously combusted. "Winner is the one who reaches the base lodge first."

He wagged a gloved index finger near her nose. "I want you to give it your all," he said. "No letting me win because you feel sorry for me."

"Sorry for you?" She laughed, completely at ease with this easygoing, wacky man. "Trust me, Mr. Sawyer, the last thing I feel for you is sympathy."

"It's Doug," he replied with a wink. "You think you can remember that? It'll make our dinner together much more comfortable if we're on a first-name basis."

"Since we won't be having dinner, I see no reason to get comfortable."

"You're awfully sure of yourself."

She practically shimmied in her boots. "Believe me, I have reason to be."

"Okay, then." He yanked his ski pole out of the ground. "Game on."

Chapter Ten

Laughter threatened to bubble from Lyn's lips, but she clamped her mouth shut around her mirth. Poor Mr. Sawyer—*Doug*—was about to find himself playing catch-up through her snowy wake.

"Shall I count off?"

The eagerness in his tone, the confidence behind the words, nearly fractured her composure. Somehow she managed to keep her enjoyment bottled up inside and give him a nod of approval.

Until the moment he shouted the word "Go!"

Emitting her usual competition *whoop,* she shot forward and hurtled downhill with the determination of an avalanche. As she gained speed on the first descent, wind slapped her nose and cheeks. The long-accustomed rhythm of decades on the slopes returned to her legs and arms, propelling her downward easily. The *scritch* of edges on ice sang nostalgic. Joy invigorated her, brought an arrogant grin to her lips. That familiar adrenaline rush flourished in her brain, and she turned to see how close Marc was behind her.

No . . .

Not Marc. *Doug.*

The visions assailed her before she could force them away. Marc's smiling face on the slopes. How his eyes crinkled when he laughed. The way he looked at night. The way he looked in the morning when he first woke up. The light in his eyes at the Oslo Awards dinner, their first real date. The dimming of that light just before she kissed him good-bye for the very last time.

Her knees faltered. The edge of her downhill ski caught a

piece of crud. She skidded, one leg up, the other down, and neither in control.

Time slowed, allowing her to experience the fall inch by inch. The air hushed. Her arms flapped, her back arched, and the skis continued sliding from beneath her. Meanwhile her heartbeat rattled her rib cage, and her pulse kicked up a notch. Or ten.

The icy ground came nearer to her floundering form. After what seemed an eternity, her left hip slammed the frigid earth with a bone-crushing jar. Stars dazzled her eyes. The breath erupted from her mouth in a pitiful mew. A flurry of ice flew into her face, pricking her cheeks below her goggles. She lay on her side and waited for the aftershocks to ease enough for her brain to reboot.

Okay . . .

Step one: Survey the damage.

Gingerly, she rolled to her other hip. Pain sprayed across her back. This was so not good. Pretty darn stupid, in fact. A thirty-five-year-old woman should not behave like a reckless teenager. Suddenly feeling every minute of her real age, Lyn brought her knees toward her chest and laid her skis one behind the other. For a moment, she remained still, inhaling one harsh breath after another.

"Lyn!" Doug's panicked voice broke from the crest of the hill.

She sighed. Caught. How humiliating.

"Good God." His skis came to a hard stop a few feet from her nose. "Are you all right?"

"I think so." She hoisted herself up to her haunches, and lightning forked through her pelvis. Collapsing to the ground again, she met Doug's worried gaze. For the first time in years, fear crept into her tone. "The hip hurts a lot. You'd better go get a sled."

"No." He flipped his goggles above his helmet. "I'm not leaving you alone here. If you can get up, we'll take it slow down the mountain—"

"And risk more serious injury to both of us?" she interjected, then winced. The pain edged her tone sharper than a frozen razor. Inhale, exhale. Try again. This time with some feigned bravado. "Trust me. It's not a good idea for me to go cavorting down the mountain with an injury, no matter how slight."

He sidestepped closer on his skis. "How bad is it?"

With a wave of her hand, she shooed him away. "Go. I'm okay. Really. I just don't think I should push my luck right now."

Crouching, he tilted his head closer. Honestly. Did he expect to read her diagnosis based on the slightest twinge in her expression? *Good luck, buddy.*

"You're sure?" he asked.

She forced herself to recline on her elbows, as if she currently relaxed on some tropical beach. The pain resonated through her teeth, but she managed a quick smile and a nod. "Yup. It's all good. Just a little stiff."

"Okay, if you say so." He shot up like a bottle rocket, slid his goggles into place. "I'll fly down there, I promise."

"Don't you dare!" At her outburst, his focus veered back in her direction. The amber tint in his lenses prevented her from seeing his eyes, but she sensed his misgivings anyway. "If you fall and injure yourself trying to get help for me," she explained, "we'll be in a lot more trouble. Take it slow and safe, please."

"I'll go fast, but safe," he amended, flashed a thumbs-up, then pushed off on his one pole.

Lyn watched him slide away, until he was lost to her sight over the next ridge. *Oh, God. Please let him hurry.*

The sky turned deep purple as the sun finally sank behind the mountains. When the last of the daylight ebbed away, the cold seeped into her bones.

Regardless of her warning, Doug picked up speed once out of Brooklyn's sight, then struggled to maintain his balance on the slippery slopes. Refrozen slush created rough terrain, and the waning light only increased a skier's difficulty in reaching the base safely.

No more than thirty seconds into his run, his skis skidded on a bald patch, and he flailed. While his brain struggled to keep calm, his heart pumped panic juice harder. After several seconds where his one arm and ski pole whirled like the Tasmanian Devil in his childhood cartoons, he managed to find his center of balance, plant his pole into the ground, and stop his stumbling forward momentum.

He stood stock-still and blew out the breath he hadn't realized he held. Every muscle trembled violently. If he chanced pressing on before regaining control, he'd wind up in a worse position than Brooklyn.

Moron, he chastised himself. *Slow down. On the slopes, and in pursuit of this story.*

This wasn't exactly what he'd had in mind when he'd dared Brooklyn to a downhill race. It was supposed to be a test. A test to see what she'd choose, given an escape route. He'd purposely offered her the chance to wriggle out from their dinner date. Knowing who she was, he also knew there was no way he could ever out-ski her. He'd hoped, though, despite his demands to the contrary, that she'd let him win at the last minute. That she'd decide she *wanted* to have dinner with him.

Yeah, so it took an ego bigger than Wyoming to think that way. But hey, he considered as he pushed off again, stranger things had happened. Especially today.

Around him, twilight faded. The goggles obscured more than protected at this stage. Again he stopped. With an angry jerk, he yanked them above his helmet.

Without the yellowish outlook that made everything seem jaundiced around the edges, he studied the shadowy ski lifts and tried to gain his bearings. Up ahead, the run forked. A weathered sign tacked to a skinny birch tree offered him the option of taking Snow Problem on the left or Snow Me the Money on the right. Both were posted as blue square trails.

He hated these cutesy "snow" names. Snow Problem. Did that mean there were lots of problems on that particular run? Or no problems?

Left or right? Which would get him to help faster?

In contrast to the rapidly plummeting temperature, a bead of sweat trickled from his hairline into his eye, stinging like a wasp. He blinked several times to ease the burn, but that only blurred his vision somewhat.

Useless. He was completely useless right now. With no trail map, no familiarity with this mountain, the wrong decision could screw him up entirely.

How far away was the first-aid station? For that matter, how far away was the base lodge? He stood like the perfect fool, in search of some kind of sign. Instead, only cold and darkness blew in.

He'd only been here a week, for God's sake. Thirty minutes ago he'd been a beginner. Now he had to ski better and faster than he ever had in his life. Better than Brooklyn Raine. Because she needed him to get her help.

The skis kept sliding forward, edging to the right. Okay. Instinct, right? Go the way the skis told him to go. Toward Snow Me the Money. With renewed determination, he pushed off for more speed.

The tips clipped the side of a bump. He wobbled, but gritted his teeth and forced himself back into an upright position. Just in time to crest the top of the next hill and stare down. A pattern of bumps gleamed on the dusky trail. Moguls.

He'd taken the wrong turn and now had to meander his way down a mogul run. In the dark. With one arm and a bunny-slope education. Terrific. Why not make it really interesting and throw in some sniper fire from the dense line of trees?

He inhaled sharply. *No time for whining, wussy-boy. You've been through rougher situations than this. Think about crawling on your belly in hot sand while bullets whizzed overhead and fiery wind pelted your face.* A mogul run was a playground, compared to that day.

Pushing his edges deep into the snow, he slowed his speed to a near crawl. With the ever-darkening night, being able to see the bumps before he hit them became more crucial than zipping through blind. He tightened his jaw and slid forward, allowing his left ski to crest the side of one mini-hill. He barely finished the turn before his right ski rode the natural incline of another bump. Then another on the left. Right. Left. Right. Left.

Beneath his helmet, his hair, soaked with sweat, plastered to his scalp. His calf muscles burned. A powerful thirst dried his throat. The bumps grew steeper now, with little room in between to ski around them. His knees absorbed the sledgehammer-like blows again and again and again. As the punishment continued, he toyed with the idea of removing his skis and walking the rest of the way. Yet, he realized that would only slow him down even more. So he pushed on.

At last the trail opened up to merge with another from the opposite end of the tree line. The two trails widened into one, which ran the length of the triple chairlift. Smooth as polished glass.

Hallelujah! He'd made it.

And not too far below, the base lodge loomed.

Gratitude renewed his sagging spirits, and he schussed the rest of the way down with ease. As he neared the base, he spotted several dark figures scurrying around the snowmobiles and sleds.

"Hey!" he shouted, waving his arm frantically. "Help! Please!"

One of the figures turned and faced Doug.

"Brook—" He cut himself short. "Help, please," he repeated. "It's Ms. Hill. Lyn? She fell on Snow Business. She needs a sled."

Immediately, the three men went into action. One yanked the chain from around the skis of the first snowmobile in the line.

"How far up is she?" another asked as he jammed a helmet on his head.

Meanwhile, the third hustled off toward the door below the Red Cross insignia.

How far? Doug considered for a long moment. Did he remember any landmarks in the area? Of course not. "Around the fifth crest, I think. Before the fork for Snow Me the Money and Snow Problem." That much, he knew without a doubt.

"What happened?"

"I'm not sure. She was ahead of me so I didn't see her fall. I came upon her when she was already on the ground."

"How bad? Is she conscious? Bleeding anywhere?"

"She says she's okay, but doesn't want to push her luck by

skiing down the rest of the way. I'm not so sure it's as simple as she tried to make me believe. Nothing broken that I can tell and no blood, but—"

The first man straddled the snowmobile, and the engine roared to life. The second man hooked a sled to the revving vehicle. The third returned from the first-aid station with a bundle of blankets and dumped them on the sled.

"Okay," the first man shouted over the noise. "We'll find her and take it from here. Thanks."

On a spit of snow, he rode away, speeding toward where Lyn lay waiting.

"Why don't you go inside for now?" The third man clapped Doug on the shoulder. "Grab something hot to drink. Kitchen's closed, but there's stuff in the employee lounge. Tell anyone who asks you're here with Lyn."

"But—"

"Go on," he said with a dismissive wave. "We'll take care of Lyn."

And didn't that idea burn him? Suddenly, he was the additional, unneeded appendage.

One thing he'd learned in the last few months: there was no such thing as an unneeded appendage.

Chapter Eleven

Lyn snuggled deeper into the soft folds of her plush pink bathrobe and forced her eyes to focus on the words in the novel she'd picked up from the inn's library. No matter how hard she tried, she couldn't concentrate on the murder mystery. Even with a roaring fire in the parlor's hearth, the ice wrap around her hip sent chills through her body. Luckily, the horse pills prescribed by Dr. Ryder in the emergency room dulled the pain to a throbbing ache. They also wreaked havoc with her eyesight, so she'd pulled out a pair of store-bought reading glasses a former guest had left behind. Still, the words on the page continued to elude her, in favor of revisiting what had occurred on the ski trail.

She couldn't help running her tumble over and over again in her head. Daddy always said reviewing mistakes on the slopes would prevent her from repeating them. Marc, naturally, disagreed. Marc thought a skier was better off putting the mistakes in the darkest corners of his mind to focus on the next run, the next day, the next race. Such divergent opinions always left Lyn to weigh the logic of each and decide for herself which option to choose. Today, Daddy's advice held more weight than a crowd of elephants.

Of all the stupid things to do . . .

As if insulted by her thoughts, her hip sent a sharp, stinging pain through her bones. She sucked in a breath until it eased.

Technically, her injury could have been a lot worse. X-rays showed no fractures or bone chips. Still, a pulled hamstring was serious enough to sideline her for a minimum of two weeks. Two *prime ski weeks.*

She squirmed in the high-backed wing chair and tossed the matching throw pillow on the floor. God, could her timing have been any worse? Why couldn't she have fallen in the spring or summer? When icing her hip would have been an excellent way to cool off. And when she didn't care about missing days on the mountain.

"You sure you don't want me to stick around till your sister gets back?"

Lyn looked up from the pillow's perch against the andirons to find Mrs. Bascomb near the foyer closet door, shrugging into her red plaid coat. The black lines crisscrossing the rotund scarlet figure seemed to move at a high rate of speed, making Lyn dizzy. Only several deep breaths restored some semblance of her equilibrium.

"Go." She waved off the older woman. *And take that nauseating coat with you.* "I'll be fine."

Hoisting her hands to her hips, the older woman harrumphed. "You shouldn't be alone right now."

The brass knocker on the front door suddenly thundered through the room.

"Apparently someone agrees with me." Mrs. Bascomb thunked across the gleaming oaken floorboards. Between the coat and her lime green vinyl snow boots, she resembled a traffic light swaying in a windstorm. "I'm guessing Richie decided to stay with you until April comes back. Thank God. You'll be in good hands, and I can rest easy knowing someone's here to take care of you."

Mrs. Bascomb yanked open the door, but Richie Armstrong didn't step inside. Nor did April or any other member of her entourage. A man crossed the threshold. Big, brawny. With a large brown paper bag in his gloved left hand. And nothing in his right. Not even a matching glove. In fact, his right hand hung uselessly at his side, mannequin-like.

Lyn blinked once, twice. How on earth . . . ? Her jaw dropped. "Mr. Sawyer?"

"Doug," he corrected as he shook the snow-flaked hood off his head.

His presence in her parlor, where he stood surrounded by

dainty antiques, delicate china knickknacks, and floral fabrics, only enhanced his masculine aura. She recalled a scene from some old movie where a former he-man wrestling star played with a little girl in a dollhouse. The wrestler looked almost monstrous in a tiny pink chair with a thimble-sized teacup in his massive paws. And yet, he also looked adorable, because his love for the child resonated so beautifully through that image. The picture, once drawn into her brain, refused to leave.

Only now, Mr. Sawyer portrayed the he-man, and her inn became the dollhouse. She, on the other hand, was no child. Self-consciousness washed her cheeks with heat, traveling down to her chest.

Despite the sudden perspiration drenching her skin, she clutched the collar of her robe and gathered the chenille fabric beneath her chin. "What are you doing here?"

"We have a date, remember?"

"A date?"

He hefted the bag into her line of sight. "Dinner. You lost the bet. I beat you to the base lodge."

Dinner? He'd come here for dinner? *Here?* Panic shot through her. She couldn't wrap her head around this situation. She had completely forgotten about Douglas Sawyer, what with her quick ride from sled to ambulance to emergency room gurney. He, however, apparently hadn't forgotten about *her.*

Her hand crept up to smooth her hair. God, could he have shown up when she looked any worse? If she dared to stand in front of a mirror right now, she'd probably see that Hallmark card character, Maxine, staring back. Complete with fuzzy pink robe and bunny slippers on her feet.

Okay, they were pink gingham booties with fur linings, but still, Lyn would have preferred a pair of strappy sandals or even some really harsh kick-butt boots. Yeah. A man who oozed machismo the way Mr. Sawyer did? He'd probably love a woman in thigh-high black leather numbers.

She shook her head at her own bizarre thoughts, and her oversize reading glasses slid down the edge of her nose. Oh, great. Maxine to the max.

But if her appearance disappointed him, he didn't show it. He simply grinned and held up the bag again. "Where should I set this up?"

A lump rose in her throat, and she swallowed hard. "You're kidding, right?"

He slowly shook his head, that quirky smile never leaving his face. "Nope. You agreed to the race. And then you lost."

How could such a large, imposing bulk of a man appear so boyish and unassuming? And so . . . appealing. He had to leave. Now. Before she agreed to let him stay.

"I didn't lose. I was injured." Which, in her opinion, nullified their so-called bet and the ensuing date.

"Just your hamstring. Not your appetite, right?"

Her brain stumbled.

Before she could form a coherent argument, Mrs. Bascomb's maple syrup tone oozed into the conversation. "Lyn, honey? Aren't you going to introduce me to your young man?"

"He's not—"

"I'm sorry." Doug ducked his head in Mrs. Bascomb's direction. "I'd shake your hand, but I'm still getting the hang of this thing." He indicated his false arm, and the fingers actually folded into the palm, as if ashamed of themselves.

Mrs. Bascomb tittered. "That's quite all right, sir."

"I'm Doug. Doug Sawyer. Ski-Hab student, current champion in a downhill race with Ms. Hill, and now, I'm her dinner date."

"Well, good for you!" Mrs. Bascomb leaned toward Lyn and gave an exaggerated wink. "Good for *both* of you."

No, no, no. The evening had just nosedived from miserable to catastrophic. As soon as she walked out the inn's front door, Mrs. Bascomb would blab this juicy gossip all over the town. For the next six months, Lyn wouldn't be able to buy milk without someone stopping her for details about the big bad wolf of a man who'd showed up at her doorstep with a take-out dinner.

"I'm Mrs. Bascomb, by the way. But you can call me Eleanor."

Eleanor? Even after all these years, after all they'd experienced together, Lyn hadn't earned the honor of calling Mrs.

Bascomb by her first name. And *Doug* got favored-nation status within five minutes?

Snap! The fire crackled, munching on dry wood in the hearth. Sparks lit up the air, then faded to bits of gray ash.

But . . . wait. Even before she dealt with Mrs. Bascomb, she had to clear up a few pertinent details with Mr. Sawyer.

Tilting her head, she studied him from a new angle. "How did you know where I live?"

He shrugged but never lost eye contact. "Ace told me you ran a bed-and-breakfast called Snowed Inn. The cab did the rest."

"The cab?"

"Well, yeah." His gaze flickered from Lyn to the door and back again. "I don't have the whole driving-with-prosthesis thing down yet. Certainly not enough to risk slippery roads and snow squalls."

"Right." Heat rushed to her cheeks. *Way to make him feel like an invalid, Lyn.* "Of course."

"Lucky for me, the driver not only knew where you live, but he knew you personally."

"He did?" Oh, God. It had to be Larry, who'd harbored a not-so-secret crush on her since she and Marc first moved here. Of course, his wife of forty-five years nipped any romantic intentions Larry had in the bud. But that didn't stop him from naming himself her Happiness Fairy, in charge of making her smile again at all costs.

"He sure did. Right down to your favorite restaurant."

Yup, that would definitely be Larry.

"So he stopped at Winterberry's Cafe for me. I hope you don't mind, but I chose lobster bisque and a grilled vegetable panini for you. Fancy way of saying soup and a sandwich. Hearty, but light. I figured the painkillers would knock out your appetite to some degree. They had that effect on me. Made everything taste like soap."

The pills might have curbed her appetite, but they hadn't completely erased her brain's higher functions. She shot a hand toward him. "Hold up. I'll grant you, Larry is a font of information when it comes to me, but he's not a doctor. So how'd you know about my hamstring? *And* the painkillers?"

Ruddy color filled his angular cheeks. "Oh, well, umm . . . let's just say your local hospital's not big on confidentiality."

She bolted upright. Pain sliced across her back, but she stifled a wince in favor of moral outrage. "They disclosed my condition to you?"

His gaze fell to his feet. "No. More like they didn't secure your chart as well as they should have."

Mrs. Bascomb's chuckles erupted before Lyn could accuse him of spying on her.

"Clever as well as handsome," the old woman remarked. "Be careful, Lyn. This one could romance your heart out of you in no time."

Through the veil of her lashes, Lyn stole a glance at his chiseled features, the boyish grin, the eagerness in his incredible eyes. Her heart somersaulted in her chest.

He was so different from Marc, so polar opposite the fine-boned European gentleman who'd swept her off her feet with soft words and candlelight. Mr. Sawyer was brash and bold, more likely to use a club and sling her over his shoulder.

And yet, he somehow plucked the same heartstrings she'd assumed would only ever play for Marc.

That was exactly what terrified her.

Chapter Twelve

Doug knew an ally when he saw one. He might have lost Ace's approval by pursuing this story, but in Eleanor Bascomb, he'd gained a one-woman army of unwavering support. And even better, an illuminated entry into Brooklyn Raine's dark well of secrets.

"Eleanor?" He held up the bag. "Since my date's incapacitated and I only work at seventy percent efficiency these days, do you think you could give me some help in the kitchen?"

Eleanor grinned. "I'd love to. Let me just take off my coat. You go right through there." She pointed to a narrow hallway with a closed door at the end. "Ignore the 'Employees Only' sign on that door and go on inside. I'll be there in a minute."

"Umm . . ." He glanced at the door, noted the latched handle, then turned back to the woman in the loud plaid coat. "I think I'll wait for you."

"No, go on—" The older woman cut herself off. Her curious gaze burned a trail from his right shoulder to the useless appendage dangling at his side. His skin itched from her scrutiny, but he steeled himself to remain perfectly still and wait. In the sudden silence, the grandfather clock behind him ticked off time in earsplitting increments.

"Slap my head and hear the rattle," Eleanor exclaimed at last. "How stupid of me. You're a Ski-Hab student, so you're still getting used to your prosthesis. I'm so sorry. Come along. My coat can wait. I'll help you inside first."

Her ludicrous neon green boots *thumpety-thump*ed across the wooden floor. As she passed him, he caught a whiff of old-lady perfume. And mothballs. The strong, noxious scent tickled his nostrils, and he sneezed. Since his left hand still cradled the bag from Winterberry's, his right hand shot up to cover his mouth. Automatically. Instinctively.

"Bless you," both ladies said in unison.

Doug barely registered their words. He paused, the palm of his prosthetic hand near his lips, the sensation strange in more ways than one.

Well, I'll be. The impulses actually work.

And the lifelike exterior really did feel like skin. Too bitter at the time, he'd paid little attention to the bio-designers who'd fussed over him, gushing about all the wondrous, up-to-date features his prosthetic arm had. Now he had an inkling as to why they'd been in geek heaven. He stared at the hand at the end of his jacket sleeve. He had to admit, the gadget was incredibly realistic looking. Right down to the fingers complete with knuckles, nails, and fingerprints. The technological world had come a long way since the days of Captain Hook. Slowly, he lowered the medical marvel to his side, almost by subconscious thought alone. Like a normal person.

Aside from their initial response, Lyn and Eleanor showed no additional visible reaction, thank God. They didn't even seem to notice his sudden bewilderment. But then, why would they? Nothing unusual to them in preventing the spread of germs and being polite in social situations.

But for him, the simple gesture was nothing short of miraculous. For him, his ability to cover his mouth when he sneezed was a cause for celebration.

He looked up, smiled, and murmured his thanks to the two women. As the flash of realization burned brighter inside him, his smile widened. With all the celebrities and sports stars he'd known, all the friends and few family members he had, he could think of no one better with whom he wanted to share this moment than Brooklyn Raine.

Of course, right now, she looked pretty zonked. Glassy-eyed, quiet, so unlike the ski dynamo he knew from years past—and a few hours ago. But that was understandable. After all, she'd been bested by the one-armed bunny-slope graduate.

Yeah, yeah. The painkillers influenced her sleepy condition, not wounded pride.

And hey. If he were the disreputable type, he could ply her with a glass or two of wine and have her entire life story in less than an hour.

"Ahem!" Eleanor's forced throat-clearing refocused his attention. "Come along, lover boy. Let's get your dinner date off on the right foot."

Lover boy? He stifled an exhale of annoyance. "Could we just stick with Doug, if you don't mind?"

Her rusty chortles echoed through the hallway, abrading his nape. "What? You've got a problem with 'lover boy'?"

Umm . . . *yeah*. Could she have come up with a more harmless nickname? He supposed it was a good thing, then, he wasn't the disreputable type.

On an exaggerated sigh, she pushed open the door. "I suppose we can stick with Doug, if that's what you prefer." She flipped on the light switch, and illuminated a room of stainless steel appliances, copper pots hanging from the ceiling, golden oak cabinetry, and miles of Corian counter space.

Wow. He'd seen smaller kitchens in army mess halls.

"Who's she feeding in this place?" he asked as he set the bag down on the nearest counter. "The NFL?"

"Well, athletes, for sure." Eleanor bustled from one set of cabinets to another, pulling out utensils, silverware, and linens. "Skiers in the winter. In the warmer months, it's hikers, canoers, and mountain climbers. This is a bed-and-*breakfast*, meaning breakfast is included in the accommodations. Lunch isn't. Everyone loves a bargain. Meals are no exception. And Lyn's savvy enough to know that a good, hearty breakfast keeps her customers happy and coming back for more. Not only that, most of our guests need a lot of fuel to handle Mother Nature's challenges here. Even the peepers have a habit of tanking up before leaving for the day."

"Peepers?" Unzipping his parka, he blinked in confusion. "What's a—?"

"Leaf peepers. The tourists who come in the fall to see the foliage."

Before he could form an argument, she reached up to his collar and yanked the winter jacket off his shoulders and down his arms.

His nose twitched at that same dangerous mix of moldy flowers and mothballs, but he held back the second sneeze to a snort.

"I know I shouldn't complain about them," she said in a low whisper.

Clearly, she'd misinterpreted the noise he'd made.

"They bring a lot of dollars into this community," she added. "*Especially* the peepers. They buy maple syrup, cheddar cheese, fruits and vegetables, bales of hay for decorating their big-city homes. Even my dime bags disappear fast during peak foliage time."

Her . . . what? "I'm sorry." He shook his head, resisted the urge to pound out whatever clogged his ears. He could've sworn she'd said . . . "Your what?"

"My dime bags." Her caustic laughter erupted again. "Change purses, silly. My craft group and I make all kinds of hand-knitted goodies to sell at fairs and local events: afghans, scarves, hats, and change purses. We started calling the purses dime bags—you know, like a bag to hold dimes—and the city people thought the name hilarious. Sort of an 'Oh, look how quaint the dumb local yokels are' secret they savored. Now we have little labels we attach that say, 'Handcrafted by the Dime Bag Knitting Club,' and we can't make them fast enough. Last year, we sold more than three hundred in October alone. Enough to pay for two brand-new range-of-motion machines for the Ski-Hab program. Those big hydra-whatevers?"

"Hydrokinesis machines." Over the last week, Doug had spent plenty of time in the wave pools used to strengthen balance and motion.

"That's them." She grinned, and her false teeth gleamed whiter than pearls beneath the dozens of hundred-watt bulbs in the spotlights recessed in the ceiling. "Bought and paid for by the quaint, dumb local yokels."

He had to admire their marketing savvy. "Very clever."

Turning, she opened an overhead cabinet. When she faced

him again, she held a pair of stoneware dishes and matching bowls. "Gerta will be in at five tomorrow, so be sure to clean up when you're through here."

"And Gerta is . . . ?"

"A terror about *her* kitchen." She strode to a walk-in pantry and returned a minute later, pushing a two-tiered silver tea cart. "If she finds so much as a crumb on her counter, she'll fillet you and serve you to the guests."

He swallowed hard. "Guests?"

Right. This was an inn. Which meant there had to be guests. Another variable he hadn't taken into consideration when he'd dreamed up this plan. How in the world could he charm Brooklyn Raine into talking if strangers kept popping into their dinner conversation?

Hand stuffed inside the bag, he leaned toward the doorway. "How many guests are staying here?"

Once again, Eleanor's cackles raked his flesh as she slipped a beige lace tablecloth over the cart's surface. "Relax. The only ones staying here this week are Lyn's sister, April, and her family. And they spent the day at Lake Champlain, sightseeing. Which should buy you"—she craned her neck to peer at the green numbers glowing on the industrial microwave—"roughly two hours of quality time with our Lyn before the troops return. Give or take half an hour."

He pulled out the plastic quart of bisque. To his surprise, the contents were still hot. "How can you be sure?"

"Because April called a few hours ago to say they were staying for dinner before taking the ride back here." She looked up from the tray top she'd set with flatware, napkins, and seasonings, and winked. "That means you have until eleven or so, depending on where they stop, what kind of traffic they hit on the road, and of course, provided Lyn stays awake that long."

"Do you help out all of Lyn's dates this way?"

She took the soup from him and pulled off the lid. "I don't know. You're the first one."

One eyebrow arched, he placed the aluminum dish with the panini onto the counter. "Like what? The first one this week?"

Eleanor's lips tightened into a thin line.

Strike one. "This month?"

Silence met him. Strike two.

The only sound in the kitchen was the *tink* of the ladle hitting the Moroccan red bowls as she poured the pink soup inside. Lumps of lobster meat crowded the creamy broth. The scent of nutmeg enticed his stomach to growl.

"This *year?*" he tried again.

She flipped the cardboard off the aluminum container almost violently. "Try 'ever,' " she retorted.

Ouch. His conscience stabbed him right between the eyes. "Oh, come on. You're telling me it's been years since anyone's asked her out?"

"No. I'm telling you it's been years since she said yes. In fact, I'd go so far as to say it's been *decades*."

The stabbing increased to jackhammer intensity.

"So, lover boy," she added, "you didn't just win a race. You won the lottery."

In the silence of the parlor, Lyn indulged her body's demand for a little shut-eye. The hum of Mr. Sawyer's low voice infiltrated her haze in lullaby fashion. But Mrs. Bascomb's raucous laughter pierced the room's harmony like a speed drill. So much for rest. Maybe if she feigned sleep, *both* her guests would take the hint and leave.

"Sit up, Lyn," Mrs. Bascomb ordered with the cadence of a drill sergeant. "Your young man's brought you dinner. And it's impolite to fall asleep in your soup."

Opening her eyes, Lyn flashed a withering glance at her tormentor in the vile red coat. The effect was probably tempered by her sleepiness, but the intent apparently registered.

Instead of aiming another zinger her way, Mrs. Bascomb focused her fussy side on the tea cart's contents. She straightened the ecru lace tablecloth, smoothed the napkins, then directed her next comment to Mr. Sawyer. "Doug, you sit over there, and I'll set the cart between you."

She pointed to the wingback chair on the other side of the hearth. When he didn't immediately jump to do her bidding, Mrs. Bascomb clapped in a staccato rhythm. "Come on, boy! Get a move on." Her sharp, owlish eyes focused on Lyn. "You too. The sooner you're both set up, the sooner I'll be out of your hair."

Lyn rolled from her side to her back, then pushed herself upright in the armchair. Pain sizzled, and she sucked in a sharp breath.

Mr. Sawyer's gaze snapped to her face. His forehead etched in deep lines, he rose from the chair. "Maybe this was a bad idea."

"Oh no, you don't." With one forceful shove, Mrs. Bascomb pushed him down again. "Something tells me you *both* need this. I'm not leaving until I know this date is in the best possible shape for you to enjoy your evening."

"Has it occurred to you that I'm in too much pain to 'enjoy' my evening?" Lyn retorted.

"*Pffft!*" Mrs. Bascomb practically spat in disbelief. "It's not like you've never pulled a muscle before. Aren't you the same woman who won the local spring downhill with a fractured wrist?"

"I was younger then."

"Oh, right. That was a whole four years ago. Before you became decrepit."

Lyn stared at the flames and pictured Mrs. Bascomb's voice box burning to a crisp in the fireplace. Honestly, she loved the old woman, but too much familiarity had blurred the lines of privacy between them. And the wrong comment to the wrong person could prove disastrous for her.

Luckily, Mr. Sawyer seemed to sense the tension and immediately jumped into the fray. "Thanks so much, Eleanor." He grasped the live grenade by her liver-spotted hand. "I'll take it from here. Why don't you head home now?"

"Ooh, anxious to be alone, eh?" She winked. "Can't say I blame you."

While Lyn simmered, he shrugged. "Well, we *are* on borrowed time."

"Okay, okay." She picked up the embroidered throw pillow from the floor and propped it behind Lyn's shoulders.

Lyn shot her a questioning look. Since when had the old lady become maternal?

"I'm leaving." Mrs. Bascomb plodded toward the front door.

"Umm . . ." Lyn pointed a shaky finger toward the kitchen. "Use the back door, please."

Mrs. Bascomb stepped back with a very audible harrumph. "I'm going to assume your rudeness is due to pain."

Pain and utter exhaustion. But also because it was less likely Mrs. Bascomb would walk around the house to sit on the porch and spy through the front windows. Tomorrow, Lyn would owe her neighbor a very big, very heartfelt apology. But for now, the sooner she left, the better for Lyn's peace of mind.

"Assume whatever you like," Lyn said on a sigh. "Just go."

Thankfully, she did. Not, however, without a lot of inaudible grumbles and the *clop-clop* of those ridiculous snow boots.

Only after she heard the back door shut did Lyn relax into the cushions of the chair. "I'm sorry, Mr. Sawyer," she whispered. "But I'm going to ask you to leave as well. I'm really not up for a date tonight."

"Okay. First off, I thought we'd agreed you'd call me Doug. And second, no pressure here, but you do have to eat. And so do I. So what do you say we table the 'date' idea and just make this about two hungry people sharing a meal? Doable?"

No ready argument sprang to her lips. The man had a point. And he'd gone through a tremendous amount of inconvenience on her behalf. How could she repay his generosity by turning him out into the cold night without a meal? A meal he'd already paid for? And honestly? He *had* won their bet, fair and square.

"Doable," she said at last.

The visible tension on his face vanished, and he pointed to the soup. "Shall we? I don't imagine this will stay hot much longer."

"Absolutely." She inhaled the sweet-salty aroma of the bisque, and her stomach growled its approval.

As she lifted the first spoonful of bisque toward her lips, she struggled to keep her wrist straight and not splash the delicate lace tablecloth. Once she'd succeeded, she looked up at her companion. And froze.

The intensity on his face chilled her already cold blood. He gripped the spoon so tightly, his knuckles bleached. When his hand sat level with his chest, he leaned forward, craned his neck at a flamingo's angle, and practically inhaled the soup.

Her stomach pitched. Had the man never eaten around other humans before? Baboons had better table manners.

But . . .

Wait . . .

Awareness came slowly. His left hand. He was eating with his left hand. Of course he was. Because since his accident, his left hand had become dominant. Or, at least, he tried to force it to be dominant.

He caught her stare and cleared his throat.

She couldn't help the pity that pierced her fuzziness. Soup. Probably the hardest food for a recent upper-arm amputee to master. But he'd known she wouldn't be able to stomach anything heartier. In spite of his discomfort, he'd placed her condition first.

Mrs. Bascomb's comment echoed in her head. *Be careful, Lyn. This one could romance your heart out of you in no time.* Turned out no time was the understatement of the decade. He'd already opened the locked cage where she kept her heart. A few more such gestures on his part and her heart would leap out to meet him halfway.

In an attempt to put him at ease, she smiled. "I guess I'll have to thank Mrs. Bascomb for using the old tablecloth," she lied. "She must have known my hands are too shaky to worry about spills."

Gratitude gleamed in his eyes as he returned his spoon to the bowl. "Why don't I put the bisque into mugs instead? We could sip instead of slurp."

"You'd do that for me?"

"No." He took her hand in his and squeezed gently. "But you're willing to appease *me*. So thank you."

For the first time since she'd left the emergency room wrapped in ice, warmth infused her. From a simple touch. "You're welcome."

Chapter Thirteen

A skilled reporter, Doug knew how to lead Lyn into revealing herself slowly. Once he'd poured the soup into more manageable handled mugs, he relaxed enough to engage her in idle chitchat. At least, for her, it was idle chitchat. But not for Doug.

He began with a casual glance at the floral curtains, Victorian-era furniture, and the glow of the fire. Next, a small, thoughtful sip from his soup mug, and then he tossed out a simple but complimentary remark. "These rooms have such a comfortable feeling."

She looked around the parlor and smiled. "They're supposed to. Most of my guests travel a long distance to get here, and when they're here, they need a cozy place to return to after a grueling day on the slopes or slamming around the white water. It's my job to make sure they look forward to returning to this inn day after day, year after year."

"Hence the hot cider on the sideboard, the classical music in the hidden wall speakers, the hurricane lamps, the quilts and throw pillows, and all the other cozy shenanigans you have going on here."

She laughed and shrugged. "All part of my evil plan."

"I'd believe that if you didn't look so angelic." Which she did. The dimming firelight, combined with the soft glow from the hurricane lamps, created a golden halo around her slightly tousled hair. The hot soup had restored some color to her cheeks and reanimated her features, negating the effects of the painkillers.

The color in her cheeks deepened. "Believe me, I'm no angel.

What I did to you yesterday afternoon should have clued you in to that fact."

"I told you, that little push woke me up, knocked some sense into me." *Got my mojo back and put me on the course for the story of the year. Maybe even the prestigious Metro Journalism Award.*

She shook her head. "I acted like a bully, and you're being gracious about it. I don't know if I could be so generous if the situation was reversed."

"The situation wouldn't ever reverse," he assured her. "At least not with me. I learned not to push girls when I was five."

"Oh?" She leaned forward, eyes bright with curiosity. "Do tell."

"Jenny Hendrix jumped off the low end of the seesaw while I was on the high side."

She sucked in a sharp breath. "Yowza. Even for a little boy, that must have hurt."

No need for him to elaborate, although he still saw stars when he thought about the pain that day.

"Yeah. Exactly. Anyway, she tried to run away, I chased her, she tripped over her own two feet, told the teacher I pushed her, and my mother was called to the school."

She sipped her soup, looking at him over the rim of the mug. "And that innocent event stayed with you all these years?"

"You've never met my mom. She was a schoolteacher herself, but she taught high school English. The word *formidable* was created to describe her."

Her eyes grew wide, or at least *wider,* considering her current dazed condition. "What did she do? She didn't hurt you, did she?"

Every time Lyn showed some minor concern for him, he had more trouble connecting her to the Coyote on the mountain. "She never hurt me. She lectured, she took away things like comic books and television time, but she never laid a hand on me."

"What about your father?" she asked.

"Out of the picture before my second birthday. Went to the store for milk one day and never came back."

"I'm sorry."

He shook off the sympathy. "Don't be. My formidable mom more than made up for the lack of a dad." And Lyn had just handed him the perfect segue. "How about you?"

"How about me what?"

"Your parents."

She turned her gaze toward the fire before answering, "Oh, you know. They're just normal parents, I guess."

"Lucky you," he remarked, but he watched her reaction closely.

She grimaced, a brief moment of pain across her features, then the return to placidity. "Yup. That's me."

Change the subject, keep her off-balance. "How long have you lived here?"

"A little over ten years now, I guess," she replied. "You should have seen this place back then. It was originally a hunting lodge."

"With all that entailed, I assume? Something like a caveman's home away from home?"

"You assume correctly. Indoor plumbing, thank God, but I don't think any room had been thoroughly cleaned since the place was built. Cobwebs everywhere, dust six inches thick, and I don't even want to remember the condition of the bathrooms."

She grimaced, from pain or the memory of what this inn used to be, he didn't know. He opted to believe the latter.

The grandfather clock on the outskirts of the room chimed once, and Doug's attention veered to the time displayed on the golden face with its laughing moon. Ten-thirty. The night was slipping away. How had *that* happened? He stared at the tea cart, the empty plates and drained mugs. Two hours had flown by in the blink of an eye. Time to knuckle under and get some real info out of the pretty innkeeper.

"It's a nice town," he remarked. "From what I've seen so far, anyway. Did you grow up near here originally?"

"No, I came from"—she yawned—"somewhere else."

A guarded response. Push forward or hang back? Oh, who was he kidding? He'd never been a hang back kinda guy. "Yeah? I went there once on vacation."

She offered a tight-lipped smile, and he pushed again. "So did 'somewhere else' have a name?"

Before she could answer, the front door swung open and slammed against the wall. On that thunderous sound, a pair of heavily layered demons rushed inside, shouting accusations about what he surmised was a broken pair of earbuds.

"There's no sound at all coming from the right side," a female complained as she swung the thin white wires in her gloved hand. "And they both worked fine before you got your grubby hands on them."

"I didn't break them," her pint-sized male companion retorted. "I didn't even use them. You probably stepped on them in the car, and now you want to blame me."

On Doug's right, Lyn sighed heavily. "And they're back."

"That's enough," another feminine voice said from the open front door. "Take off your coats and boots and put them in the closet. Then go upstairs. Quietly. Don't wake Aunt Lyn."

"It's okay, April," Lyn called. "I'm awake. We're in the parlor." As if in reply to Doug's unspoken question, she offered an apologetic smile and whispered, "My sister and her family are here for the week. Normally, the kids aren't such monsters, but I'm guessing a full day of togetherness took its toll."

In other words, reinforcements had arrived. Interview over for tonight. He rose. "I should probably go. Would you mind calling me a cab? Meanwhile, I'll get the kitchen whipped into shape so Gerta doesn't fillet me for your guests tomorrow."

He turned the tea cart around to more easily push it into the kitchen but was nearly bowled over by a woman racing into the parlor.

"Lyn? What are you doing up at this hour?"

The woman wore a bright turquoise ski jacket, unzipped to reveal a thick sweater in a softer powder blue shade, and dark denim jeans. She'd apparently paused long enough to remove her shoes because she slipped inside on stocking feet. Well, sort of stockings, anyway. They were more like gloves for feet, with each toe in its own separate compartment and each compartment a different color. His gaze took in the wearer of these bizarre but childish socks. She was petite, even smaller than Lyn. A pixie really, with reddish-brown flyaway hair, and glossy brown eyes like a teddy bear's. She looked nothing like Lyn, and yet, he could easily peg them as sisters. Their speech patterns, postures, and take-control attitudes all indicated some shared DNA.

The woman strode past Doug and aimed straight for the chair where Lyn sat huddled in her fluffy pink robe. Once she reached her sister's side, she crouched. "Are you okay? What happened?"

Lyn waved a dismissive hand. "I took a tumble on the slopes. Pulled my hamstring. No biggie. I'll be fine in a couple of weeks."

"It's my fault," Doug said. "I dared her to race me."

On a gasp, the woman swerved to face him, lost her balance, and fell on her bottom. Slowly, she rose, rubbing a hand over her disgraced posterior. "And you are . . . ?"

"Exaggerating," Lyn answered with an emphatic head shake. "April, this is Doug Sawyer. Doug, my sister, April."

"Nice to meet you." Quickly, he thrust out his left hand.

"Same here." April blinked several times, and then clasped his left hand in hers.

Doug had learned early the best way to head off the embarrassed reactions from those unaware of his prosthetic hand was to beat them to the awkward.

"April?" A man's voice came from the foyer.

"In the parlor, Jeff," April called back.

Within seconds, they were joined by a dark-haired man who'd not only removed his shoes but his coat as well. He too wore a sweater and jeans—in coordinating shades of gray and black, respectively. His socks, however, were normal lightweight ski socks. With all five toes on each foot sharing the same woolen compartment. Thank God. Doug didn't think he'd be able to keep his mouth shut after seeing a man in multicolored, multitoed socks.

Once again, Lyn made the introductions, but this time, Jeff beat Doug to the handshake stage, and Doug was forced to use his prosthesis. If Jeff noticed anything bizarre about the false hand, he made no visible reaction. Which meant he was either oblivious or super-polite. Either way, Doug exhaled a sigh of relief.

With the pleasantries out of the way, the room grew silent and strained. The only sounds came from the Mozart concerto playing subtly in the background and the tick of the pendulum in the grandfather clock.

Finally, Doug ventured into the stillness. "I should see about these dishes."

April's gaze swept the contents of the tea cart, then swerved to Lyn. "Did we come back at a bad time?"

"Of course not," Lyn replied. "Doug was with me when I fell. And knowing I'd spent the evening in the emergency room, he brought me a late dinner."

Both April and Jeff swerved their attention to Doug. Recognition tickled Doug's memory. Something about them, the way they stood, Jeff with his hand possessively placed on April's shoulder, seemed so familiar. Where had he seen these two before?

Nope. Not a clue. For now, he shook off the wispy images.

"I've overstayed my welcome, anyway," he said, "and your sister was too polite to throw me out."

"Not true," Lyn said. "Unfortunately, I wasn't exactly the most scintillating companion tonight. I'm surprised I didn't put him to sleep."

Now Doug shook his head. "Not possible. But for tonight, our date has come to an end. I wanted to ask you—no pressure, mind you—but since you won't be able to ski for a few weeks, maybe you'll drop by the Ski-Hab area Friday afternoon? Say . . . after four? We could try for something more closely resembling a real date? Where I take you out to a nice restaurant? For a better meal than soup and a sandwich? If you're feeling well enough, that is."

Lyn hesitated. "I don't—"

"She'll be there," April jumped in. "I'll drive her to the mountain myself."

Doug didn't know how he'd managed to win over the sister

so quickly, but he wasn't about to question his luck. "Great. So if you'll excuse me, I'm off to the kitchen to clean up the mess, and then I'll hit the road."

"April, do me a favor?" Lyn pointed at Doug and the cart. "Could you help him with the dishes? You know where everything goes."

God, no. He'd rather fumble alone, thankyouverymuch.

"Don't be silly. I have everything under control."

"But . . . with your arm . . . I mean, the prosthesis . . ."

Instantly two pairs of eyes veered to stare at his right arm. Great. *Thanks for bringing my infirmity to their attention, Lyn.* All the more reason to avoid an audience in the kitchen. Last thing he needed was someone gawking at how the cripple managed to wash dishes.

"I've had hundreds of hours of occupational therapy," he insisted, "which included dishwashing and general housekeeping. You just take care of the cab, and I'll take care of the kitchen. Deal?"

"No deal." Lyn folded her arms over the wide lapels of her fuzzy robe. "You're at a disadvantage, not knowing where Gerta keeps everything."

"Lyn has a point," her sister announced. "Gerta's a tyrant about her kitchen. I'll just come along to make sure everything's in the right spot. Trust me. If you don't place the saltshaker at the proper angle with the pepper shaker, ol' Gert will skin you alive."

"Surrender, Doug," Jeff said with a grin. "You can't win against these two."

Before Doug could form any additional argument, April took the tea cart by the handle. "Come on. It won't take long." Once he'd followed her out of the parlor and toward the kitchen, she craned her neck to add sotto voce, *"Date,* huh? And a follow-up on Friday? How'd you manage that?"

When Doug stepped into his slopeside condo an hour later, Ace Riordan's head popped up over the back of the sofa. "Where have you been?" Every sharp word sliced the air.

"Gee whiz, Mom, you didn't have to wait up for me." He unzipped his jacket and opened the closet door.

Ace's icy glare could turn the condo into the Arctic Circle. "And you're not answering my question. Where were you?"

He offered the kid a smug grin. "I had a date."

Blue eyes narrowed to cobra slits. "With whom?"

"The proprietor of a certain bed-and-breakfast." While Ace swallowed that horse pill, Doug hung his jacket in the closet.

"You didn't."

He leaned out, the picture of innocence. "Didn't what?"

"Dude." Ace slammed a fist into the sofa's top. "I told you to leave Lyn alone."

"Since when do I take orders from you?" Doug headed for the kitchen, where the package from Jake lay waiting on the counter, silently beckoning to him.

"Since I pulled a lot of strings to get you into the Ski-Hab program. Now you're gonna screw up everything by pursuing a story no one cares about except you."

"Oh, I don't know about that." He found a steak knife in the kitchen drawer and carefully split the packing tape along the top of the box. "I spoke to Jake Hardwick, and he agrees with me that this could be the story of the year."

"So you'll ruin a woman's life for 'the story of the year.' Great."

"Lighten up, Ace. You know me better than that. Since when have I ever ruined anyone's life? I've already told you. I'll make her look like the patron saint of amputees."

Ace unfolded his body from the couch and clucked his tongue. "Wow. You still don't get it, do you? It doesn't matter that you're not one of those hacks from some gossip rag. For Lyn, *no* publicity is good publicity. All she wants is to be left alone. Why can't you respect that?"

"Because it's stupid." He flipped open the flaps.

"Says you."

Doug pointed a finger in Ace's direction. "Good comeback. You got me there. But guess what? You haven't changed my mind."

He pulled out the sleek black laptop and wireless device sitting inside. Time to power up this sucker. He wanted to start recording his perceptions and the details of today's events while they were still fresh in his mind.

"Oh, now I get it," Ace retorted. "You didn't just lose your arm in that Humvee accident. You lost your soul too."

Doug looked up from his new box of toys and offered a joyless grin. "I'm a reporter, Ace. We have no souls."

"You *did*. Before Iraq. The Doug Sawyer I used to know wouldn't sell out like this."

"I'm not selling out. I'm writing a great story about a great woman. It'll put this little mountain and Ski-Hab on the public's radar. Let everyone know about what goes on here, which in turn could mean lots of donations to keep the program running. What's so horrible about that?"

"Because it's not what *she* wants. It's her life, her story. Don't you think she should be the one to decide whether or not you share it with the world?"

With the laptop plugged in and the Wi-Fi signal strong, Doug pecked the name Brooklyn Raine into the search engine. A list containing dozens of pages of information popped up. He started with images: Brooklyn on the medal podium at the Olympics, on a Disney castle float with Marc Cheviot at her side, on a cereal box. All familiar to his memory, but very different from the woman who ran Snowed Inn. The last image he found was taken outdoors, where she stood beneath a heavy black awning. The caption read, "Brooklyn Raine leaving the funeral of her father and coach, Alan Raine." The headline above the corresponding article screamed, DADDY'S GIRL NO MORE.

Ouch.

Wincing, he scanned the byline. Lorenzo Akers. Doug should have known. Akers was the muckiest of the muckrakers. An oily snake who played to the lowest common denominator. Without reading it, Doug knew how the article would slant. Akers loved to breathe life into nasty gossip and innuendo. If Lorenzo Akers was indicative of the type of reporter Brooklyn Raine had come up against in the past, Doug couldn't blame her for shying away from the press.

"You're not even listening to me, are you?" Ace's accusation brought him out of his reverie.

"Of course I am," he lied. "I'm just not heeding you. There's a difference."

Ace yanked the cordless phone off the wall mount and turned his back to keep it out of Doug's reach. "You know what? Fine. Let's see how much access you'll get to her when she knows who you are and how you came to be here."

Doug leveled a steely gaze at the kid. Time to lay down the cards. "You're going to admit your culpability in that? And Richie Armstrong's? Which do you think will hurt her more? My intention to write a positive story about her and her program or the betrayal of two men she's always considered friends?"

Ace's complexion turned candy apple red.

"Go to Canada, Ace," Doug ordered softly. "You've got a competition to prepare for."

Lips drawn into a tight line, the kid shook his head. "I'm not leaving as long as you plan to write this article."

"I'll tell you what. I'll let you read the article before I send it to Jake. You can have first approval."

"Give *Lyn* first approval," Ace said. "Before you turn the article over to Jake or anyone else at *The Sportsman,* let Lyn read the article and give you her approval."

"Okay, fine. I'll let her read it first."

"*And* give her approval to the publication," Ace reminded him.

"Yeah, yeah. Fine. Whatever you say."

"No, not whatever I say. I won't let you weasel out of this later due to some stupid technicality you dreamed up. I want you to repeat after me, 'Before I allow *The Sportsman* to print any information about Brooklyn Raine or Lyn Hill, I will tell her personally who I am, what I've done, and allow her to have final approval on the article.'"

Doug smirked. "Cute."

"Say it."

"It's really not necessary—"

"Say it!" Ace's shout nearly rattled the windows.

"I've already said—"

"'Before I allow . . .' Say it right now." Ace waved the phone overhead as if he'd just discovered the Holy Grail. "Say it, or I'll call her and tell her everything."

So Doug did.

Chapter Fourteen

For the first time in aeons, Lyn slept until late morning. When she finally left her bedroom and hobbled into the dining room, she found the sideboard already cleared, except for a beautiful spray of a dozen bloodred roses interspersed with bright purple irises in a cut crystal vase. The soft floral scent filled the air with more appeal than her normal heated cider redolent of pungent spices.

Near the glass and golden-oak hutch filled with bone china, April sat at the head of the table. In her hand, she held a ceramic mug with the phrase BLACK DIAMONDS ARE A GIRL'S BEST FRIEND in bold black script. She smiled over the rim and nodded toward the colorful bouquet. "Nice, aren't they?"

"Beautiful." She flashed a knowing grin. "What'd Jeff do or say to compel such a grand gesture?"

"They're not from Jeff, and they're not for me. They're for you. There's a card attached, if you care to look."

She stared at the arrangement again. For her? Who on earth . . . ?

Doug. Of course. They were for her. From Doug.

Turning the vase, she found the small yellow envelope sticking out from the plastic spear sign holder among the blooms.

With the unopened card in hand, Lyn limped toward the spindled first mate's chair to April's right.

"Should you be up and walking around?" April asked with all the authority of an older sister.

"Don't fuss." She waved a hand in dismissal, and the envelope crackled in the air. "Besides, you know I can't lie in bed all day."

"Yeah." April grinned. "The bane of lazy days, the Raine work ethic. Do you think our great-great-grandmother was one of those women who gave birth and went back to plowing the fields an hour later?"

"Probably." Easing her aching muscles into the chair, she attempted a smile but wound up grimacing when the pain sprayed across her back yet again.

"How's the hip?"

"Stiff. But I'll live. What's for breakfast?"

April pushed back her chair and rose. "I'll tell Gerta you're awake and hungry. She made pumpkin pancakes today. Even drew jack-o'-lantern faces on Michael's using chocolate chips. God, I love that woman! If you ever decide to fire her, let me know first, okay? I'd hire her for Rainey-Day-Wife in a heartbeat." She bent close, pushed the hair from Lyn's cheek, and peered at her, maternal concern crinkling her forehead. "You okay?"

Lyn nodded. "Just coming out of the painkiller fog."

"Hang tight. I'll get you a cup of coffee, and Gerta will bring you breakfast. Then we'll force-feed you another pain pill, and you'll be foggy all over again. So enjoy clarity while you can." She disappeared into the kitchen.

Clarity. Yeah, right. Lyn sat with her elbows on the table-top, her head cradled between her hands, and the envelope lying before her. Curiosity burned, but cotton had replaced the brain in her skull. Her eyes were still too blurry to read so much as the florist's name and address.

April was right about one thing. Coffee would definitely help.

"Here we go." Sure enough, April came back with two mugs full of caffeinated comfort. "Skim milk, no sugar for me." She winked. "I've got a wedding dress to fit into."

Lyn reached for the second mug.

"Half-and-half for you, right?" April tenderly took Lyn's hand and placed the mug inside her curled fingers. "Got it?"

Lyn nodded. "You should have been a nurse."

"I'm a professional mom. Plays into the job description."

April sat beside her again. For several minutes, neither

spoke as each sipped and allowed the brew to jolt them into the day.

After a while, the silence of the house permeated Lyn's fuzzy head. "Where is everybody?"

"Jeff took the kids to the mountain for the day so you and I could have some 'alone time.' "

Lyn quirked a brow. "And why exactly do we need 'alone time'?"

Under Lyn's scrutiny, April's gaze focused on the words emblazoned on her mug while her fingertips toyed with the curved handle. "That depends on you."

Uh-oh. April's sudden aversion to looking her in the eye didn't bode well. "C'mon, April. Speak up. Gimme the details. What's planned for me today that I'm not going to like?"

"Well . . ." She sipped the coffee, smiled again at Lyn over the rim. "I figure we can either call Summer to ask for her help with my wedding . . ."

"Or . . . ?" Lyn waited for the other shoe to drop.

"Or we could talk about your date last night."

Ka-thump.

April's eyes brightened as she fidgeted in the captain's chair, clutching the armrests as if to keep from leaping into the air. "Who was that guy? And why didn't you tell me you were dating again? Not that I'm not thrilled. Believe me, I am. It's long past time you put away the grieving widow routine. And this Doug guy's adorable. In a big, bad lion-with-a-thorn-in-his-paw kinda way. Did you meet him at Ski-Hab? How'd he lose his arm? Did you see his prosthesis? It's totally realistic. You could barely tell it was fake. He says it has fingerprints and everything."

Lyn rubbed the pads of her fingertips over her closed eyelids and sighed. "April. You're rambling."

A flaw only Jeff found endearing. For everyone not currently engaged to April, including Lyn, her runaway mouth had the same effect as nails on a chalkboard. Particularly when she honed in on a topic no one else wanted to discuss. Like Douglas Sawyer.

"Oops." April slapped four fingers over her mouth. "Sorry. I guess I'm nervous about calling Summer."

"Why? I'd imagine she'd be thrilled to help you. This is right up her alley: planning, organizing, bossing you around." Lyn laughed, but April didn't join in.

"Let's get back to your *date*," April said with a feral grin. "I see you haven't opened your card yet."

Amusement fled abruptly, and Lyn frowned. "I'm not ready."

"What's to be ready for? It's a card. And I'm dying to see what it says."

Another sigh escaped Lyn's lips. "You have no boundaries, do you?"

"Oooooh. Testy, huh? That means this is more than just a date for you. It's a relationship."

"It's *not* a relationship. For heaven's sake, we just met two days ago. And how would you know what my testiness means? If I was, in fact, testy?"

"Trust me. You're testy. And I know what that means, thanks to Jeff."

She briefly closed her eyes so April wouldn't notice her pupils rolling into the back of her head. "Just because you're marrying a psychologist does not make you an expert on people."

"That's not what I meant."

Sarcasm slipped out easier than a third sigh. "Do tell, oh wise and gifted one."

"Okay, I will. You really like this guy. And that scares the bejesus out of you."

"Nope."

"Liar." The accusation slipped between them easier than a dryer sheet under a door. "You can't fool me, Lyn. I've been there. When I first started falling for Jeff, the idea scared me stupid."

"I'm not—"

"Yeah, you are. Scared stupid. Just like me. For different reasons, but the reaction's the same. See, I kept thinking about my first marriage. All the times Peter cheated on me and A, did I want to go through that agony again and B, what if he cheated because I was boring? How long would it be before Jeff found me boring?"

"I am *not* boring."

"Yeah, you are," April repeated with a toothy grin. "But that's beside the point. Those were *my* issues. Your issues are different."

Lyn folded her arms over her chest and glared. "So what are my issues, Dr. April?"

April shrugged. "Only you know for sure, but I bet one of them is, 'What if I fall head over heels for this guy and he leaves me? Like Marc did.' "

"Marc didn't leave me."

April's features softened, as did her tone. "Yeah, sweetie. He did. I admit, it wasn't his choice. But he left you. And then *you* left you. You holed yourself up in this inn and built a wall around your heart. But now, this Doug guy's climbing over your wall. And you're scared stupid."

And April came waaaaay too close to the truth for Lyn to continue this discussion. "You know what? If I want analysis, I'll talk to Jeff."

For the first time since she'd arrived at the inn, April frowned. "Please don't. He's a stickler for patient confidentiality, so if you talk to him, I'll never find out if I'm right."

"Does it matter? Even if you're wrong, you won't admit it."

"But I'm right, aren't I? You met two days ago. You shared an intimate dinner last night. He sent you that gorgeous gaggle of flowers this morning. And you haven't even looked at the card because you're 'not ready.' That means this guy's pretty special to you."

"In the first place, I'm not ready because I'm still too bleary-eyed to focus. Second, our so-called 'intimate dinner' was soup and a sandwich, for heaven's sake. Practically lunch."

"Uh-huh. And Friday night?"

Lyn sipped her coffee. "There is no Friday night."

"There most definitely will be a Friday night."

"Twenty minutes ago, you had me confined to bed."

"Until you reminded me you don't like to sit still." April

pointed her teaspoon like a proctor's baton. "This is life, Lyn. Welcome back, we've missed you. The thing is, you don't just take a chance when you play Monopoly, kiddo. You've got to seize the joy out of every moment, suck life dry. Life's been sucking you dry for too long. So if you're not confined to bed, you're going out with Doug. Besides"—she beamed brighter than afternoon sun on pristine snow—"I already promised I'd drive you there."

April was so revved up, she wouldn't listen, no matter how logical the argument. Okay, so if she wouldn't listen to Lyn, maybe she'd listen to someone else.

"I think," Lyn said slowly, "it's time to call Summer."

The good thing about going anywhere with Jeff was that he didn't expect Becky to stay with her little brother all day. In fact, after two runs when they first arrived, he cut her loose. As long as she met them for lunch at the lodge at one, she had free access to the mountain without Michael as her constant companion. Thank God. She couldn't exactly talk to guys with the twerp around.

Becky wasn't looking for a long-term relationship, or even a romance. She just wanted to hook up with a hot guy for the week. Someone to take a few runs with, to share some laughs and make this week bearable. Most of all, someone who'd look really good in the photos she'd take. So her friends wouldn't pity her for missing winter break in Cancun, thanks to this family trip.

Once out of Jeff and Michael's visual range, she pulled the cherry lip balm from her inside jacket pocket and rolled it over her lips. Pretending to inspect her board, she watched the skiers and boarders lining up near the triple chairlift for possible companion candidates. A few couples, several junior high–aged boys, and a guy with a purple-and-green-striped jester hat on his head. Pass.

With a calculating eye, she began her mental scrutiny of the males loitering around the base area.

Loser, double loser, loser extraordinaire . . .

Ah! There! Lone guy headed for the triple chairlift. Could

be cute. Hard to tell with the helmet covering most of his head and face. But he had more potential than anyone else so far. He would definitely require closer inspection. She strode to the lift, her snowboard tucked under her arm, then meandered toward the line for singles only, right behind her target. Mr. Potential didn't look in her direction, so she faked a kitty-cat sneeze.

That got him to turn around, at least long enough to murmur *gesundheit.*

She flashed a perfect smile. "Thank you."

Shoot. He already faced front again. Before she could get a good look at him, and he could get any real look at her.

Becky inched closer to the guy, so close that if he whipped his head around, his lips would smack her forehead dead-center. Time to open up a conversation.

"Ummm . . . excuse me?"

He didn't move.

Cute but stupid? She could work with that if she had to. Not her first choice, of course, but if he turned out to be a good-looking zero, she'd take a bunch of pics this morning and then ditch him by lunchtime. So long as he didn't have that faraway look: the farther away, the better he looked.

Becky was just about to tap the guy on the shoulder when she heard, "Hey, it's you."

Turning, she found herself face-to-face with Ace Riordan. He stood outside the black-strapped queue, goggles and helmet dangling from his left hand and his board held against his right hip.

Heat rocketed up from her throat to her cheeks. *Oh God, oh God, oh God.* Not him. Not again. Not after their last meeting when she'd called him a perv. And made a total idiot of herself.

"Becky, right?" he said. "You're Lyn's niece."

Funny. He didn't seem angry or insulted. More like . . . interested. In her? Why?

She tried to speak, but croaked instead. Her mouth felt more clogged than the lint filter in her dorm's dryer. Swallowing hard, she nodded.

"Are you headed up to the summit?"

"Uh-huh."

"You any good on that thing?" He jerked his head toward her pink camo snowboard.

Another nod.

"Mind if I ride along with you?"

"Why?" The word escaped before she thought better of it.

He shrugged. "Why not?"

Because you're you, and I'm me. This time, though, she managed to keep the comment behind tight lips.

"Come on." He ducked under the black barrier and popped up beside her on the other side. "Slide over to the two-or-more lane."

"Hey!" someone behind Becky interjected. "No cutting."

Ace smiled, his teeth whiter than the snow covering the trails around them. "Sorry. We'll move to the back of the line, okay?"

His words still hung in the air when the first squeal of recognition erupted. "Omigod, you're Ace Riordan!"

With a sidelong wink at Becky, he replied, "Guilty as charged."

On sharp gasps and dull whispers, the crowd rushed forward in a frenzy. Cell phones and digital cameras popped up at every angle. Elbows jabbed her back and ribs. Boots stepped on her toes. The crush of people jerked her left, yanked her right, and pushed her backward, all at the same time. Shouted requests pierced the air.

"Ace, can I get a picture?"

"Why are you here, Ace?"

"Would you sign my jacket?"

A wooly mammoth of a man suddenly threw his weight into Becky, and she stumbled. Oh God. She'd be trampled to death under this mob. A swift hand shot out to grip her elbow, keeping her upright. Ace.

Her snowboard slipped from her grasp, fell to the slushy ground, and became lost in the sea of boots surging to reach the world-famous Snowball.

"Easy guys," Ace shouted, to be heard over the roar of

requests. "Cut my girl here a little slack. She's not used to this kind of attention."

He wound an arm around Becky's waist, hauled her up against his side. Annoyance took a temporary backseat to safety, and she clung to him.

"My board," she whispered. "It's on the ground."

Ace gave her a surreptitious nod. "Okay, okay, everybody do me a favor and take one giant step backward, please."

Like an army of robots, the clamoring fans retreated enough for Becky to scoop up her now totally scuffed board. Once she held it high enough to inspect thoroughly, her spirits sank to new depths. A jagged crack ran between the bindings. Great. She must have tutored jock-for-brains Isaac Morgan more than a hundred hours to earn the money for this board. Now it was garbage. Tears of frustration filled her eyes, but she sniffed to hold them in check.

Bitterness burned her throat as she switched her focus from the ruined snowboard to Ace's grinning face. Why had he popped up here all of a sudden? She should have known he had some ulterior motive for paying attention to her. Like the great Ace Riordan would ever want to spend time with a nobody like her.

The harder she tried to stifle her emotions, the more ragged her breathing grew. "You know," she managed to say over her tremors, "I'm really sorry I insulted you the other day. But at least, when I did it, I had no idea who you were. And I thought I was protecting my brother. But this?" She held up the cracked board. "This was just plain mean."

One last shove against his shoulder, and she stalked by him, headed against the flow of the throng—*away* from Ace Riordan. As far away as she could get.

Using her broken board to part the crowd, she zigged and zagged past the eager fans until she finally broke out of the queue. She should have gone to Cancun, should have told her mother she needed to stay on campus, should have opted to spend the week with Aunt Summer or Grandma rather than come on this stupid trip.

"Hey!" Ace called over the melee. "Wait!"

Becky only increased her speed. Any minute now her anger would surrender to her despair. And she'd *die* before she'd let him see her cry.

"Becky! Wait up!"

She ignored him and kept going. After leaving the ruined snowboard against a battered steel trash can, she thudded across the outdoor deck. She nearly collided with a family exiting the lodge when she yanked the handles of the double doors. With a quick dodge and a mumbled "Excuse me," she fled inside.

The noise level indoors slammed her like a brick wall, along with the odors of oily food, smoky wood from the fireplace, and sweaty old socks. Naturally, there wasn't a chair or inch of table space available to sit and sulk. Going downstairs would mean walking past the ski shop with all that shiny, top-of-the-line equipment displayed in the windows.

She had no interest in visiting the lame game room again, and she wasn't old enough to go upstairs to the bar area. For now, she meandered through the crowds, bypassing customers holding disposable cups of hot chocolate, coffee, soup, or chili, and avoiding tripping over boot bags and duffels lined up on the outskirts of the aisles between tables. Everyone seemed to be laughing or talking excitedly or just plain having a good time with friends and family. Everyone except her.

And today was only day three! She'd never make it to the weekend without her board or her headphones, which Michael had ruined yesterday. Forget her cell phone. Mount Elsie was the black hole of dead zones. She was stuck in solitary confinement until Sunday night.

On a dramatic sigh, she thunked over to the cafeteria area. Maybe she could drown her problems in a hot chocolate and a soft pretzel. With some of that nacho cheese sauce for dipping. Carb City, the perfect place to cure the blues. The line wended from the tray and silverware area, past the information booth, and almost to the back of the lodge. Oh well. It wasn't like she was in a rush. She had hours to kill with nothing to do.

Reaching the line's end, she slid behind the last customer

and proceeded to wait. The heat from the fireplace behind her seared through her jacket, but with no place to stuff her gear, she suffered in silence.

She'd barely moved up two spots before a voice murmured in her ear. "Hey."

Whirling, she met Ace Riordan's heart-melting smile with a growl. "What? You're not done ruining my day?"

"I'm sorry about your board."

"Yeah, I'll bet."

"No, really." He took her hand. "Come on."

She pulled out of his grasp with a jerk that almost made her tumble, but she managed to steady herself by slamming her knee against the edge of a bench. Fabulous. All this and bruises too. Who could ask for anything more? With one hand rubbing her abused leg, she ordered, "Go away."

"Will you just come with me? Please?"

"Why? You have fans lurking in a dark corner to grab me and shave my head?"

He had the nerve to laugh. "God, you sure get your back up easy."

"No one's making you stay here," she retorted. "So go away and leave me alone. Then we'll both be happy."

"Sorry. No can do. I'm not leaving until you agree to come with me."

Frustration escaped in a long hiss of expelled breath. "Where?"

"Just follow me."

"Fine," she exclaimed. "Make it fast."

He took her hand and squeezed when she tried to pull away again. "Be a good girl and play along, Becs. Can I call you Becs?"

"No." Because when he called her Becs in that husky way, butterflies flitted in her stomach and her toes curled in her boots.

"Too bad."

Never releasing her hand, he pulled her downstairs, past the rest rooms, the locker rooms, and straight for the ski shop. As they neared the entrance, she hung back. Now what?

Maybe he really did have a bunch of fans waiting to attack her for what she'd said to him the other day.

"Come *on!*" Ace pulled harder, and she stumbled, landing clumsily against his chest.

Their awkward entrance drew the attention of two people behind the counter. "Hey, Ace," a tall, gawky young man with a tremendous overbite exclaimed. "What's up?"

"Dennis," Ace replied, "meet Becs. Becs, this is Dennis. And he's going to outfit you with all brand-new equipment. At my expense. Pick whatever you like. Then you and I will hit the summit and tear this place up."

Chapter Fifteen

In mid-pedicure, Summer Raine Jackson whipped her ringing cell phone from her Coach bag. She glanced at the caller ID and smiled at her friend Laurel in the chair beside her. "It's Lyn," she said as she hit the connect button. Without a hello, she spoke into the mouthpiece. "Don't tell me April's driving you crazy already!"

"Hey, thanks, Sum." April's sarcastic edge could have sliced Summer's ear in half.

Whoops.

Embarrassment lowered her voice to a hush. "April?"

At Summer's question, Laurel winced and sucked in a breath.

Ignoring her friend's reaction, Summer moved straight into crow-eating mode. "I'm sorry. I just . . ." What? What could she possibly say that wouldn't sound petty or mean? She just knew how Lyn valued her peace, and April, complete with entourage, left a trail of chaos wherever she went? Yeah, that'd go over well.

"Relax," April said with a giggle. "I'm busting your chops. No offense taken. In fact, you're probably right, to some small degree."

Summer did a double take for Laurel's benefit. Cupping the speaker, she whispered, "Forgot. This is the new and improved April."

"Ah, yes," Laurel replied in the same low tone. "April in lurrrrve, living in her pretty pink world of hearts and flowers."

Summer still had trouble believing her older sister now had

115

poise, self-confidence, and a man who adored her. All the wonderful things Summer, herself, *used to* have.

She hastily shut the door on those thoughts, as she had every day for over a year. "So how goes the vacation?"

"Great. Lyn's got a boyfriend."

"What?" Lyn? Now even the eternal grieving widow had a more exciting love life than she did? "Are you serious?"

In the background, Lyn squawked, but April spoke over whatever argument Lyn wanted to make. "He's a Ski-Hab student. Big guy. Great eyes. And those eyes get all googly over our baby sister."

"Pay no attention to her, Sum!" Lyn's voice carried from the background. "She's delusional."

"Saw it with my own eyes and so did Jeff," April rejoined. "Came back to the inn last night to find them cozied up together with dinner for two and a fire in the hearth. Very traditional first date kinda stuff."

Sort of like what Summer planned often these days. Except she usually wound up dining alone. Brad's late nights at the office occurred frequently. Too frequently for her to ignore the warnings that screamed in her head.

No. Don't go there.

Her gaze dropped to her bare feet where Helen, the nail technician, rinsed off a gritty lemon-scented paste and revealed silky smooth skin beneath. Summer forced another smile in Laurel's direction and held up two fingers as if to say, *Give me a couple of minutes.* "So did Lyn reciprocate those googly eyes?"

"She tried to play it cool, but couldn't quite pull it off. Especially when he asked to see her again on Friday. I think it's safe to say our Lyn is finally out of mourning."

Muffled fumbling resonated through Summer's phone and then Lyn's shout, "Never mind all that. Ask April why she's calling, Sum."

Okay. "I have to admit, my curiosity is piqued. What's up, April? I'm guessing you didn't just call to tattle on Lyn."

"Umm . . . no." Uncertainty crept into April's tone. "How are you, Sum?"

Uh-oh. Summer heaved a disgruntled sigh.

Helen looked up with startled eyes and held up the nail polish applicator. "Not right?"

Summer waved a hand and flashed a thumbs-up at the dark-haired woman. "No," she whispered. "The color's fine. Perfect. Really."

Unlike the rest of her life.

But if April opened a conversation with idle chitchat hesitation, whatever she intended to say probably wouldn't sit well. Which explained why she had Lyn there for backup.

Summer stiffened in the black leather massage chair, despite the "magic fingers" attempting to knead tension from her shoulder blades and lower back. "I'm fine, I think," she replied with caution. "At least, so far."

Laurel must have caught Summer's sudden change in mood because she leaned forward, brows arched questioningly.

Summer waved her off. "What am I missing here, April?"

"Well, I . . . umm, I wanted to ask you—no pressure, mind you—but I was just sort of wondering . . ."

"Oh, for heaven's sake!" Summer had no idea what reaction her outburst had on April, but Helen snapped up so quickly, she smeared strawberry margarita nail polish across two of Summer's toes. "Spit it out."

"Iwaswonderingifyoumightwanttohelpmeplanmywedding." The statement came out in one breath, one long word. Unintelligible gobbledygook where all Summer heard for sure was "I" and "wedding."

"Could you say that again, please?"

"Wouldyouhelpmeplanmywedding?"

A tiny thrill rippled through Summer, but she forced herself to remain calm. "Once more, April. And this time, take a breath or two in between words."

Instead, April laughed. "Yeah, yeah, I get it. You really want me to squirm before you give me an answer."

"No. I just want to make sure I'm hearing you correctly." Because inside her, a little girl was screaming, *Yippee! A wedding!* But the cynical, more adult Summer needed confirmation before she allowed the little girl free rein of her emotions.

"Yes, you are," April replied, her smile evident in the return to her natural cadence. "Look, you and I both know if I run this show on my own, it's gonna turn into a fiasco. Ordinarily I wouldn't care. What I mean is, if it were up to me, I'd do a quickie ceremony, little house party afterward, nothing fancy. But, since Jeff and I met through *Taking Sides,* the show wants to broadcast highlights. Everything from the planning to the ceremony and the reception. I managed to draw the line on letting the talk show's audience choose my wedding gown. Still, this wedding has to be bigger than I can manage. *And* perfect. And I'm soooo far from perfect. As you often remind me."

"April . . ." Lyn's cautionary chastisement came through loud and clear, meaning they must have switched to speaker phone for the big moment.

"Relax, Lyn. Summer knows what I mean. Anyway, Sum, if I'm Princess Chaos, you're the Czarina of Control. You know exactly what to do and when to do it. Nothing would *dare* to go wrong on your watch. If I place the details in your hands, I know you'll make sure that everything runs smoothly. Just like your wedding. No doves, mind you." Panic laced that last directive. "No birds at all, in fact. I mean, I'm not entirely certain what exactly I want yet, and of course Jeff will have some say as well . . ."

While April droned on and on incessantly, Summer pulled the phone away from her ear.

"What's up?" Laurel asked in a whisper.

"My sister just asked me to plan her wedding."

"April? The one you said doesn't like you?"

"I never said she didn't like me."

Laurel arched a cryptic brow.

Okay, well, maybe she had. But that was then. Before April had tossed her this very precious lifeline. "We just don't see eye to eye that often."

"And you think you'll see eye to eye on wedding plans? How do you know she won't become Bridezilla?"

"April?" Summer whispered back. "Puh-leez. There's nothing 'Zilla' about April." That had been her problem for years: lots of drive, no backbone.

"I don't know," Laurel replied airily. "All that fame, the reporters following her everywhere? You don't think she considers herself better than everyone else?"

"April?" Summer snorted. "No way."

After *Taking Sides* and Jeff had entered her life, April had become a different woman. The new and improved April. But, thank God, her ego—or lack thereof—had remained the same.

"Summer?" April's faraway voice drifted out of the phone. "Are you there? Did we lose you?"

She fumbled with the cell, putting it back to her ear. "I'm here. I'm just . . . stunned, I guess."

"Stunned in a good way?"

"Yes, I think so." In fact, the more Summer considered the prospect, the more she liked it. She needed the distraction, and maybe in spending more time with two people so wildly in love, she might find the formula to put her own marriage back on the till-death-do-us-part path. Otherwise . . .

No. She wouldn't consider the alternative.

"I *love* the idea," she said with forced enthusiasm. "I'll give you and Jeff the perfect wedding day to send you off into your happily-ever-after."

And hopefully, she could find a new happily-ever-after for herself at the same time.

For the next two days, after therapy sessions and ski lessons, Doug would race back to his makeshift office setup. He'd commandeered the breakfast nook as his temporary desk with his laptop plugged in and the high-backed bench as his chair. Once as comfortably ensconced as possible in such an environment, he'd power on and delve into his research regarding Brooklyn Raine.

On Wednesday, he easily ignored any guilt that pricked his conscience for digging into her private background. He'd always believed in the media's right to information. Celebrities, in exchange for wealth and fame, had to sacrifice their desires for anonymity.

But on Thursday, the voice inside his head shouted too loudly to be dismissed. Lyn Hill/Brooklyn Raine shook his beliefs regarding fame to the core. A lot of her wealth, and most likely her late husband's as well, had been poured into the Ski-Hab program. Lyn Hill lived quietly and simply. She didn't do public appearances, didn't court the press in any way. Her ski gear didn't scream advertisements for any brand names. No patches on her jacket pushed the newest energy drink or the latest innovation in thermal underwear. She didn't own a string of slopeside condos or any major real estate holdings, except for her bed-and-breakfast, which had a resale value far below that of his apartment in Manhattan.

What he'd dug up should have thrilled him. Both his reputation and his promise to Ace hinged on an article that shed a positive light on Lyn and Ski-Hab.

Unfortunately, one question eluded him. A question crucial to any good story: Why? Why give up the sports spotlight and dump all your money—your *future*—into a program for injured war veterans?

He dismissed most of the usual reasons. Obviously she wasn't looking for positive publicity, or publicity of any kind for that matter. He found no evidence of court-ordered community service or a need to clean up her image. She didn't seem to be involved for political reasons. So . . .

Why?

Among the links he'd bookmarked he found a copy of the interview that Ace had brought to his apartment months ago. Now he watched it again, this time without a pharmaceutical cocktail muddling his brain and skewing his perception.

As he studied the news item this time, with his personal Ski-Hab experience fresh in his mind, shivers trickled down his spine. The Marine who talked about "ending it all" struck a deep chord. Doug squirmed on his bench while he listened to the wounded man's plan to steal pills or slice his wrists or just hope that death might come for him in the middle of the night.

How close had Doug come to that ledge? Too close. If not for the interference of his mother, Ace, and in an odd way, Lyn, where would he be right now? The shivers increased to an ice bath, leaving him chilled from head to toe.

Focus, Sawyer.

He paused the video, took several deep breaths, and pushed away the dismal thoughts of his former misery. Fate had given him the opportunity to make a new start. A start even the great Giles Markham hadn't received. How dare he consider, for one second, throwing that gift away?

His left hand gripped the fingers of his prosthesis. A heartbeat later, the fake fingers on his fake right hand not only curled. They actually *felt* the touch, sensed the chill that had taken over his extremities. Amazement jolted him. Whether he wanted to accept this miracle or not, the nerve endings in his shoulder were doing exactly what the prosthetic experts had predicted. With renewed purpose, he hit the play arrow on his laptop screen, sending the news item bursting to life once again.

". . . The program was begun several years ago by a group of local skiers when one of their own arrived home without a limb during the first Gulf War . . ."

Stop.

Bingo. *One of their own.* One of Lyn's own? Like a brother or a cousin? Someone who needed the special skills of a sports rehabilitation program? He toyed with the idea, mentally flipped it and folded it and curled it into a dozen different shapes. The end result remained the same. A woman like Brooklyn Raine, who'd been coached by her father and devoted to her husband, would definitely give up every dime she had for a family member.

Time to dig into the family background. See if he could learn the identity of the mystery relative.

But as he clicked on link after link, frustration grew. He'd already scoured most of the information available about Brooklyn, with no mention of other family members besides her father.

On a hunch, he typed "April Raine" into his search engine.

And nearly slid off the bench when a page popped up with a list of more than fourteen thousand results.

Who in the world was April Raine? Curiosity burning, he clicked on the first link and began to read.

Chapter Sixteen

Once again, Doug paused at the top of the last hill on Snow Can-Do. Slipping his goggles away from his eyes and over his helmet, he feigned the need to catch his breath. Without the amber tint of the lenses, the mere slip of late-afternoon sunlight seemed too bright and transformed figures into shadows. At least a dozen skiers flew past his skewed vision, aimed for the inevitable line to board the lift and squeeze in that final run of the day. The wind, low but evident all afternoon, now bit into any bared skin with icy teeth.

When his vision finally cleared, he scanned the clusters of people loitering outside the base lodge.

On a spit of snow from her skis, Kerri-Sue pulled up beside him. "Nope. She hasn't shown up yet."

Doug offered her a blank stare. "Huh?"

"Lyn. That's who you're looking for, right?" She grinned. "I heard about what happened the other night. Real smooth, bringing her dinner."

His jaw dropped. "How did you . . . ?"

"Small mountain." She spread her arms wide, the extension of her ski poles encompassing the entire vista of steel gray sky, white snow, and green pines. "*Lots* of nosy residents. And Mrs. Bascomb is the biggest gossip in the county. I'd imagine the whole town knew about your date before you even had dessert that night."

"We didn't have dessert," he mumbled.

A movement near the row of Adirondack chairs caught his eye. He stared hard, hoping to discern something familiar in the figure who stood alone among the groups of friends and families. The slightest tilt of her head, a subtle gesture of pushing a curl of hair from her face, a laugh, any of the dozens of unique characteristics that made Lyn . . . Lyn.

"You know, Romeo." Kerri-Sue poked his shoulder. "You might want to play a little harder to get."

"Am I that obvious?"

"Not to Max." She pointed up the mountain with one of her poles.

Doug turned in that direction and blinked. Not once, but three times. Still, the image remained. The skier might have escaped notice, except for the traffic-cone orange caution bib plastered to his chest. But on a mountain fraught with injured and handicapped skiers of all types, Max wouldn't necessarily stand out. His companion, on the other hand, might cause a stir. A thick, black Labrador retriever trotted alongside the man, barking to direct each turn of the skis.

"A skiing eye dog?" Doug quipped.

Kerri-Sue snorted. "Cute. But I'm betting even Shiloh's noticed your obsession."

"Shiloh?"

"The dog."

"Uh-huh. I got that. I just wondered about the name. Why Shiloh?"

The force of Kerri-Sue's laughter could start an avalanche.

Doug frowned. "What's so funny?"

"Anyone else would have been curious about Max before we discussed the dog. Something like, 'Is that guy really blind?' or 'Isn't that dangerous?' But not you."

He shrugged. "I've seen blind skiers before. But with human guides. Shiloh's the first dog guide I've seen on a ski slope."

"You've seen blind skiers before." She didn't phrase the statement as a question, but she gave him an X-ray look, as if she could see straight into his insides.

Compressing his lips into a tight line, he remained mute. He'd probably already said too much.

She waited. A beat, maybe more. Finally, she gripped her poles and bent forward. "Come on. Let's finish this run. Then I'll buy you the nonalcoholic hot beverage of your choice while you change your boots. We can hang out in the lodge until Lyn shows up. Just try not to look so pathetic, okay?"

With his goggles replaced over his eyes, he pushed off on his lone pole and began the last series of slaloms to the lodge.

Pathetic? Hardly. Not when he considered where he was six months ago. Or even three weeks ago, when he first arrived here. He'd nearly come to blows with the physical therapy staff, his instructor, and Brooklyn Raine. He cringed when he thought about how much energy he'd expended to prove them wrong when all he'd needed was the right woman to prove them right. No, not the right woman. The right *story*.

Now every turn of the skis made him stronger, more secure, and ready to tackle the enigma that was Lyn Hill/Brooklyn Raine.

Keeping up his speed, he bypassed the lift line that led to another trip up in favor of the wooden tripod ski racks on the fringes of the base area. He pulled to a stop and used his pole to pop his bindings, releasing his boots from the skis.

Seconds later, Kerri-Sue pulled up beside him. "Congratulations." She clicked open her bindings, then bent to gather her skis. "I gotta tell you, I had my doubts about you when we first started. But you turned out to be one of my best students ever."

She probably told every student the same thing, but Doug basked in the praise anyway.

"Come on." With their skis and poles locked to the rack, they clumped up the wooden staircase to the lodge's outdoor deck. "I could groove on a hot chocolate myself. How about you?"

He suddenly felt the dryness in his throat and, despite the frigid temperatures, replied, "Something cold."

A sudden shriek stopped their conversation, and Doug swerved his attention to a growing crowd encircling something or someone at the edge of one of the lift lines.

"Look over there." She pointed a gloved finger toward the triple chairlift. The circle of people clamored, jumping, reaching cell phones and cameras in the air. "I'm guessing they just found your pal Ace."

"I'm surprised it took them so long."

She expelled a generous breath through pursed lips. "I'm surprised it took *him* so long."

"What do you mean?"

"Come on. He's your friend. You should know how he uses his fame to impress the girls. Same routine every time he's here. He keeps a low profile when he first arrives until he finally finds his flavor of the week. Then, suddenly, he's pulling some sweet-faced girl away from the crowd with an 'Easy there, everybody. My girlfriend's not used to this kind of attention.' About as subtle as a ten-pound bag of quarters to the face, but the results are the same. Poor girl's seeing stars. At least till the end of the week."

"And at the end of the week?"

"He's on to another ski resort and another girl." Cocking her head, she studied him with a hardened expression. "Which begs the question, how on earth can you be friends with such a shallow, callous boy? You're more than a decade older. I don't get it."

"Oh, well, maybe that's because you don't really know the parameters of my relationship with Ace."

"And they are . . . ?"

None of your business.

Hmmm . . . Probably not the best reply. He'd have to stick with the same story he gave to Lyn. Safer that way, anyway. The fewer lies he told, the stronger his disguise remained. "Ace and I aren't friends. We're more like business colleagues."

"Yeah, that's what Richie said when I asked him too. And that tells me a whole lotta nothing." Her eyes glittered like ice chips. "Maybe I should just Google you."

He kept his face a mask of nonchalance and shrugged. "Go ahead. If you dig deep enough, I bet you'll learn all the nitty-gritty details. Really important stuff like the name of my kindergarten teacher, my grade-point average in college, and my shoe size."

"Actually, I learned a lot more than that."

His limbs itched to squirm, but he dug in his heels—literally and figuratively. "Oh? Found out my favorite movie too?"

"Not quite. Did you know there's actually a reporter for *The Sportsman* with the same name as you?"

The dryness in his throat spread to his bloodstream, and sweat broke out on his neck. But he kept his expression bland, his tone light with a lilt of conversational surprise. "No kidding?"

"No kidding. Got me curious. So I called *The Sportsman*'s office. Know what I found out? Seems *that* Doug Sawyer's been on hiatus after a Humvee accident in Iraq."

"Wow. That's quite a coincidence."

"Ya think?" she retorted. Shaking her head slowly, she sighed. "You know, ordinarily, I'd kick your butt from here to Montpelier. But Richie Armstrong is no idiot. He would have checked you out thoroughly before giving you the green light for the program."

"So?"

"So I'm gonna let it go for now. But . . ." Expression hard as granite, she bounced an index finger near his face. "Watch yourself. Obviously you're here because you need to be here. And like I said, despite your rocky start, you've become one of my best students ever. Now you and Lyn seem to have something going between you, which is nice. *If* it's for real. If it's not for real, this town will take you apart piece by piece."

If Lyn stood any closer to the lodge's enormous natural riverstone hearth, her hair would catch fire. Already, smoke clung to her ski jacket and sweater. Despite the blaze of heat behind her, shivers racked her bones and prickled her skin. Her stomach flipped like a member of Cirque du Soleil. Even with her gloves off, her palms dampened with sweat. The buzz of a hundred conversations occurred around her, but she barely heard them over the thunderous pounding of her heart.

Only two things could stir up these symptoms. And flu season was still a month away. The blood in her veins effervesced, making her feel lighter than air.

She owed this topsy-turvy feeling to the man she'd just spotted seated in the lodge. Admitting her attraction, even if just to herself, released a tremendous weight from her shoulders. If she stood on a precipice right now, she knew she could fly.

Perhaps his size drew her gaze to him immediately. Douglas Sawyer was built like a professional linebacker yet moved with graceful purpose. Kerri-Sue sat beside him, her expression stern while she attempted to hold what Lyn assumed was an in-depth conversation. If Doug was listening to whatever Kerri-Sue attempted to tell him, he did so while he scanned the throngs at the lunch tables packing up their gear.

His eyes found hers and locked there as a wide smile spread across his cold-roughened features. Never allowing his focus to stray from her, he rose. Sidestepping the extended legs of skiers who removed boots, duffel bags packed and ready for departure, and coolers of iced drinks, he strode straight for her.

The closer he came, the warmer she grew. His hazel gaze, bright and intense, bathed her in strong golden sunlight. Finally, he stood in front of her, the Big Bad Wolf now resembling Prince Charming.

"Lyn." He bent and kissed her cheek.

A spark flashed in her heart, then skittered like a lit fuse through her veins. "Doug."

"I'm glad you came."

So am I.

Kerri-Sue, out of breath, stopped behind Doug and poked her head out from around his waist. "Oh, thank God you're here. If he stopped at the last hill on Snow Can-Do to look for you one more time, I would have skewered him on my ski pole. You'd be having Doug kebabs for dinner."

Lyn's sappy side, long dormant, woke up warm and eager. "He was looking for me?"

"For at least the last hour," Kerri-Sue replied. "Trust me. *I'm* glad you came."

The windburn on his cheeks made discerning his flush nearly impossible, but even in the dim light and dark wood paneling of the ski lodge, Lyn noticed the subtle change and melted a little more.

"That seems to be the general consensus," she admitted.

"Besides, if I'd dared to *try* to back out, my sister would have dragged me here by my hair."

He looked around the large open room. "Where is your sister? Kerri-Sue and I should probably thank *her* too."

Lyn giggled at the disgruntled way he said Kerri-Sue's name. "April's somewhere outside. Wanted to hook up with her fiancé and kids. They're here to ski, and their vacation week is almost over."

"Well, you two have fun." Kerri-Sue waved her walkie-talkie. "Doug, I'll radio one of the guys to stow our gear in the Ski-Hab center until tomorrow. Me? I plan to show off what an idiot I am. In public. I've got a meeting with my son's math teacher tonight. The kid's barely skidding by, grade-wise, and I'm no help at all. I can do the basics: adding, multiplication, division. Once Nate started bringing home Greek theories and square roots, I was lost."

Another sigh, a pathetic headshake, and Kerri-Sue shuffled off toward the employees' lounge, leaving Lyn facing Doug.

His eyes captivated her—sometimes green, sometimes gold—but always appraising and approving. Her shivers had disappeared, replaced with the languidness of a sauna's warmth. Time stilled. The noisy lodge dissolved into a cozy oasis for her and Doug alone.

Alone with Doug in a room crowded with après-skiers. How on earth could he make her feel like they were the only two people in this lodge with just a look?

Finally aware that they simply stood and stared at each other like empty, mismatched bookends, Lyn shook herself out of her stupor and filled the silence. "So . . . what do we do now?"

He blinked and cleared his throat. "Would you mind coming back to my condo with me? At least so I can get Norm?"

"Norm?" Her happiness aura cooled several degrees. Had she somehow mistaken his invitation? Did he plan to set her up with a friend?

He shook his head. "Not Norm like Norman. Norm like normal." He grabbed the cuff of his empty sleeve and wagged it near her. "Before we have dinner, I'd like to attach my prosthesis."

Rather than restoring her excitement, his admission only depressed her more. "You still think the lack of an arm makes you abnormal?"

"No." He unzipped his heavy jacket. "But I'm betting you're not wearing a ski bib and four layers of clothes underneath your coat. The prosthesis is just the beginning. I'd also like to get out of this gear and into some regular clothes. In fact, I wanted to run something by you. And please, if it makes you uncomfortable, say so."

The chills returned, weak but evident. "What?"

For the first time since he'd strode toward her, he looked away, focusing his attention somewhere above her. Or beyond her. Definitely not *at* her.

"Well," he told the stone hearth, "like I said yesterday, I'm not really comfortable behind the wheel just yet. Which is why I thought it might be better if your sister dropped you off here today. But I didn't really think it through. Because I hate the idea of you going home by yourself in the dark after dinner. So I thought, if it's all right with you, we could go to my place and order something delivered. Then Ace could drive you home afterward."

She didn't know whether to be touched or humiliated. Was he really concerned about her welfare, or did he have some other reason to suggest they spend the evening with Ace? Maybe after their last date, he thought she'd bore him silly. Sure, between the long day and the painkillers, she hadn't exactly been the most scintillating dinner companion. But she'd slept until well after nine this morning and had even skipped her afternoon prescription dose, preferring to deal with the occasional twinge of pain rather than a continuous cloudy, fuzzy feeling.

Maybe he worried that they had too little in common to maintain a decent conversation? The hotshot sports rep and the provincial little innkeeper? Of course, they had more in common than he knew. He had no idea she was more than just the owner of a rural bed-and-breakfast. Which, of course, was her fault. She wondered how he'd react if he knew who she really was. Not that she'd tell him.

Or . . . would she? Could she trust Doug with her secret? The idea terrified her, but logic chastised her. For heaven's sake, the man worked for Ace Riordan, a celebrity whose star burned far brighter than hers these days. Besides, by now, who really cared about her anyway? Maybe Mrs. Bascomb was right.

Here she stood, on the border of uncharted territory. For too many years she'd hidden away, buried her heart. Now, oddly, this complex giant of a man had found a way to reach her. Did she want to meet him halfway? Because if she did, she'd have to be honest with him. About her past, who she used to be.

She had to tell him. Tonight.

"Lyn?" he prompted.

Still pondering her own dilemma, she hesitated. "Umm . . ."

"Ace won't be there for dinner," he said suddenly, reminding her of the topic of their conversation. "He'll probably be wining and dining some poor unsuspecting girl with stars in her eyes. At least, that's what Kerri-Sue believes. But he's usually back around ten, if that works for you. And since I have Ski-Hab accommodations, all the local restaurants offer delivery. Anything you want, from Alpha-Bits to zeppoles."

Alpha-Bits and zeppoles?

He'd rehearsed this speech. No one came up with Alpha-Bits and zeppoles at the drop of a hat. Which meant, despite his "only if you're okay with it" speech, he really wanted her to agree to his request.

She thought back to their last dinner, also a take-out meal in a private location. The scene with the soupspoon took center stage in her mind, followed by his comment moments ago about getting "Norm," and the mental lightbulb clicked on. He still wasn't comfortable in public with his prosthesis.

Her heart wept for his insecurity, and she blinked to clear sentimental tears from her eyes. Offering him her brightest smile, she exclaimed, "That sounds perfect, actually. Not the cereal or the sugared dough balls, but maybe we could come up with something in between?"

Relief eased the tension lines around his eyes, and his confident grin returned. "Order anything you wish. If the restaurants around here don't have it, I'll have it flown in for you."

Chapter Seventeen

Doug held her hand as they strolled through the miniature village of boutiques and art galleries that separated the ski area from the slopeside lodgings. Evening had already devoured the last slice of sunlight. Replicas of carriage lanterns on arched steel poles illuminated the walkways in a soft lithium glow.

In honor of the upcoming holidays, decorative evergreens planted in waist-high wooden hogshead barrels twinkled with the glow of white fairy lights. Instrumental Christmas carols played from speakers hidden in artificial poinsettia plants and fiberglass deer. Roasting chestnuts cloaked the more natural, clean sting of snowy air.

"Every time I walk through here, I feel like breaking into a chorus of 'It's a Small World After All.'" Doug cocked his head in her direction. "You know? From the ride at Disney World?"

With a wistful smile, she nodded. Yeah, she easily understood the comparison. Cedar A-frame buildings with open gingerbread scrollwork and Pennsylvania Dutch hex signs over the doorways were supposed to make the tourists think of some rustic Scandinavian ski town. But since Lyn had spent oodles of time in rustic Scandinavian ski towns, she thought the architects had simply taken every quaint detail from a dozen different mountainous areas and created a mishmash. Or some weird Hollywood version of Alpine life. *The Sound of Music* meets The Sundance Film Festival.

She stared at a young couple standing in front of a glass-enclosed case of gears that boasted the ability to create a souvenir from a coin. Put in fifty-one cents and get back a flattened bit of copper with a vacation scene stamped into it. Judging by the way the woman stood with her hands on her hips and her companion's equally combative stance, the two couldn't agree on what scene should be pounded into their penny.

She shook her head. Hmm . . .

On second thought, most of the tourists had the same point of reference as the architects. So she bit her lip and swallowed her distaste while she walked through this little homage to the almighty dollar. One thing life had taught her—don't sweat the small stuff.

"Have you ever been to Disney World?" Doug asked.

She shrugged. "Sure. I took my niece, Becky, when she was six or seven."

Despite her conversational tone, the memory punched her in the gut. After Michael was born, she'd offered to take Becky on vacation as a favor to April and Peter. At least, that was what she told anyone who asked. She had taken Becky off their hands so they could figure out how to deal with Michael's problems. But the truth, which Lyn had suppressed for years, was far uglier.

April had announced her pregnancy around the time she and Marc had learned the severity of his cancer. Envying her sister's good fortune, Lyn couldn't bring herself to find a sliver of happiness for April. Unfortunately, Michael's birth, and the devastating diagnosis, left them all reeling. Guilt pounded Lyn's conscience day and night. What if her negativity had brought this massive misfortune on April and Michael? Unable to face her sister, or the poor infant who'd borne the sting of her jealousy, Lyn had swooped in to take Becky out of town without ever stopping at the hospital to see her new nephew.

Yet, a few years later, when Lyn kept her vigil at Marc's bedside in Sloan-Kettering's intensive care unit, who showed up first to lend support and an extra pair of hands? April. Who came every day, brought food, offered to run errands, and generally became the shoulder for Lyn to cry on? April. April with the heart wider than an ocean. Dependable, reliable, endlessly forgiving April.

"Something wrong?"

Doug's question snapped Lyn into the present, to the village square beneath the Black Forest–style clock tower, where she'd released his hand and stopped to stare off into space. Into the past.

"No. I'm fine." At his continued scrutiny, she shook off the bitter memories with a violent shiver. "Just cold."

"Come on." He took hold of her hand again, squeezed her fingers. "Let's duck inside one of these shops for a minute."

He pulled her toward the etched glass door below a red-and-green-striped awning that bore the name Bear Necessities. Since he seemed in no rush to release her hand, she sidestepped to take the lead. She turned the latch and pushed open the door. With a tinkle of sleigh bells, they entered the shop. The smell of turpentine nearly knocked her to her knees.

Around them, like an ursine dragnet, stood hand-carved wooden bears. Hundreds of them. The thick dark sculptures reflected every possible moment in a bear's daily life, from first yawn and stretch to curling up for sleep at the end of a grueling day in the forest.

Doug stopped to gape at a ten-foot bear on its hind legs, front paws stretched upright and mouth opened to reveal sharp, pointy teeth. "Do people really buy these?"

Lyn bit back an indulgent laugh. The tourist market made little sense to those who lived in the real world. "Yes. Burt Jennings, the sculptor, makes quite a good living from this store alone. He also does ice sculptures. In fact, every year he creates a Winter Wonderland in town to raise money for Ski-Hab. It's amazing. Giant angels with wings that form arches over the cobblestone path. You walk beneath those wings and it's like you've stepped into another world. Forget Disney World. There are fairy tale castles guarded by toy soldiers, nutcrackers, ballerinas dressed up to perform *Swan Lake*. All carved out of blocks of ice. We should take a ride over there after dinner. It'd be worth whatever grief Ace gives us, trust me."

She practically bounced on her toes in anticipation. Honestly, she couldn't help herself. Something about the intricate designs Burt carved in ice, glimmering under the night sky and a few thousand watts of light, brought out the wonder-eyed child in her.

"We could go now if you're not in any rush to eat," he suggested. "You think your favorite taxi driver's available?"

Even the mention of Larry wouldn't dim her excitement. "If he's not, one phone call will make him available. Fair warning, though. He's sort of sweet on me. Once he sees us together, he'll grill you into revealing all your secrets. Make sure you're good enough for me."

"I think I can handle it." He tilted his head and studied her. "You really are the small town darling, huh?"

She flipped her hair over one jacketed shoulder. "I guess so."

"Ever been to the big, bad city, Lyn?" The lilt in his tone suggested he teased her.

The big bad city? If he only knew how many big bad cities she'd visited, competed in, and slept in. She was a veritable George Washington of the ski circuit. But the acidic memories scalded her throat and tongue.

Dropping her gaze to the dirty nutmeg-colored carpet at her feet, she swallowed the pain. "Which one? I've been to lots of cities. Montpelier to check out other bed-and-breakfasts, Boston for the symphony, even New York a few times for the theater. But none are home. Not like here."

As if he sensed she needed a subject change, he released her hand to grab the manila price tag that dangled from a string tied to the hulking bear's left paw. One quick glance at the number in bold black marker and he sucked in a breath, then winced. "Work with me here a sec. Suppose I wanted to buy this thing."

She did a double take. Him? "Why?"

"Well," he replied, "I was just telling Ace yesterday that the one thing missing from my apartment in New York is a giant ferocious-looking bear."

She laughed. God, how he made her laugh!

"What?" He cast her a quizzical glance, eyes wide and brows raised in mock confusion. "They're very popular in Manhattan. Bears are the new low-tech burglar alarms. I hear the mayor's ordered two for Gracie Mansion."

"Funny." She tilted her head, studied him from a new angle, noted the twinkle in his eyes, like fireworks. "Nope. Uh-uh. Sorry. You don't strike me as the bear sculpture type." From day one, she'd never considered Douglas Sawyer as bear material.

"Oh? And what type do I seem to you?"

A wolf, maybe. In fact, she might even consider commissioning Burt to design one of these sculptures for her, a prince emerging from a wolf pelt. But she'd never admit that to him. Instead, she ran her palm over the head of a bear with a fish dangling from its jaws. "A phoenix?"

He shot a gloved index finger, pistol-style, her way. "That's a Ski-Hab answer."

She paused, her hand resting between the bear's ears. "A Ski-Hab answer?"

"Yeah. It's one of those nice little platitudes you and the Ski-Hab staff say that's supposed to encourage the whiners like me to keep trying, keep fighting the good fight."

"I never called you a whiner." But she did think it when she first saw him. If the squirmy reaction in her feet didn't betray her, the rush of heat flooding her face was bound to give her away.

He chucked her under the chin. "Judging by the color in your cheeks, I'd say you're feeling guilty. You shouldn't, you know. I'm excelling at the whole Ski-Hab experience, thanks to you knocking some sense into me. Kerri-Sue says I'm the best student she ever had."

Kerri-Sue told every student that, but Lyn kept that comment locked behind a smile.

"How did you get involved with Ski-Hab? Did you have someone close to you in the program?"

She picked up a small carving of a bear floating in a blue glass lake, stroked a fingertip over the rounded brown belly. Doug had just provided her the perfect opportunity to open up and explain how the program wouldn't exist without her. Because of who she was. Or who she had been. But old habits died hard, and the words stuck in her throat.

Instead, what came out was, "I have a friend whose son was the first participant."

"Really? Who was he?"

Aaron Bascomb, Mrs. B's only son. But she didn't feel right discussing his story without permission, so she shrugged with a careless air. "A guy who grew up here. Came home from the first Gulf War missing a leg. A bunch of us worked with him to give him back some level of independence. When the skiing not only got him used to his prosthesis, but also improved his outlook, Richie Armstrong decided we had to continue the program for others. The rest, as they say, is history."

His face fell. Did he know she had something to hide? If he suspected anything, he didn't contradict her. He simply took her hand again. "I'd say we're reasonably warmed up. Let's go find that cab."

She shook her head. "No. You want a chance to change and get Norm. So let's head to your condo first." *Give me a chance to find some courage. Find a way to tell you the truth before the lies become insurmountable.* "We'll eat and then hit the Wonderland."

"Whatever you say," he replied. "Tonight, you're in charge."

Lyn didn't know if that made her dilemma better or worse.

For the rest of the walk, she remained deep in her own worries. She had to tell Doug about her past. About Brooklyn Raine. But how? And when? She'd never divulged this information before. Not to anyone who mattered. Most people either knew, like Mrs. Bascomb, or didn't, like most of the soldiers in Ski-Hab, who were probably still in diapers when she was at the height of her celebrity. Doug was an anomaly.

And how exactly would he take the news?

Her father's voice chastised from the Great Beyond. *Don't do it, baby. You know how people react to your celebrity. Before long, he'll be looking for handouts and favors.*

But Marc's logic argued, *He works for Ace Riordan, Lynnie. If he wanted to take advantage of someone's wealth and celebrity, Ace is a much better target. I know you're scared, but don't let your fears cloud your judgment. Go for this.*

You've been alone too long. I never expected you to mourn me forever.

Her brain spun in a vacuum of questions and self-doubt. Whose advice should she heed this time?

Me, Dad insisted.

Marc only blew exasperated air in her ear in reply.

"Almost there." Doug's voice pierced the fog of ghosts. He led her inside the locker room for the Andiron Condominium residents, past the row of locked skis and wooden benches meant for removing gear, to the automatic doors that would take them to the bank of elevators.

The hallway's creamy walls, cut crystal sconces, and taupe carpet wore a tired air. Or maybe Lyn's mental calisthenics—jumping from this life to the other side and back again—had exhausted her senses. By the time the elevator doors opened, she'd made up her mind. She'd tell Doug the truth tonight. Not during dinner—the man had a tough enough time dealing with his prosthesis and utensils. Add this bombshell, and his head would probably explode.

Okay, that was a weak excuse. But courage didn't just magically appear because she'd decided to follow Marc's advice this time. So she'd cling to her anonymity for as long as possible. Feel Doug out about a few things before she spilled her guts. Like if he could forgive someone who'd deceived him since their first meeting.

The elevator doors slid open, and Doug placed his hand against the jamb until she boarded, then pushed the button for the fourth floor. Her belly flipped as the car jerked for the ascent. Through the veil of her lashes, she studied the man beside her. Would he forgive her? Would he be willing to move into something a little more than friends? What if he decided he couldn't become involved with her? Because she'd lied? Or because of who she really was?

God, she was such a mess over him. How had he managed to pierce her armor in such a short time? Simply standing close to him released butterflies through her bloodstream. She became a teenager again, hoping her crush would ask her to the prom. Not that she'd ever gone to the prom. Bouncing from ski resort to ski resort, her adolescence wasn't exactly the normal suburban upbringing.

She'd known Marc on the circuit for years before considering a real date with him. They'd cultivated a friendship first. Of course, she'd been fourteen when they first met, and Dad never strayed from her side on social occasions in those days. Still, she'd been given ample opportunity to know Marc and become comfortable with him before they were ever alone together. They'd shared the spotlight, the ski world, and all that their fame and money could provide. Theirs had been a charmed life, a charmed romance, a charmed marriage. Too short, but charmed.

Doug, on the other hand, was an entirely different animal—in physical stature, in background, in interests, and probably in the financial realm. Yet, he had won her over in less than a day. Simply by being who he was. The one quality he had in common with Marc, a lack of guile. No ulterior motives that Dad would fret about. With both men, what she saw was what she got. In many ways, he saw himself as ruined, imperfect without his right arm. Perhaps that was why he appealed to her. He shook her out of the cocoon she'd wrapped around her heart, made her realize that, like him, she'd allowed her loss to paint her as broken. Useless.

With Doug, she woke up after years of some sleep-life. A grief coma. No wonder the town called her the mourning glory. All the old platitudes murmured for years by well-meaning friends and relatives ran through her head.

Get back on the horse.

Just because Marc died doesn't mean you did.

And her personal favorite from, naturally, April. *You don't just take a chance when you play Monopoly, kiddo.*

Well, apparently, she was finally ready to take that chance again.

The elevator's chimes announced they'd reached their destination, and the doors slid open.

As she followed him down another tired cream-colored hallway, she bolstered her reserve. Yes. She'd tell him tonight. Take a chance. Dare to grab for another shot at love.

Inside the condo, when Doug took her coat and turned toward the storage rack, Lyn's gaze lit on his makeshift office setup on the kitchen counter. Despite her numb fingers and icy cheeks, she bypassed the warm living room with its cozy furniture and gas fireplace. She headed straight for the laptop, printer, and other paraphernalia. "You've been working?"

In three long-legged strides, he cut her off before she could round the counter's edge. "Just testing out my prosthesis."

And obviously embarrassed by whatever clumsy attempts he'd made. Well, she'd have to put him at ease. Assure him she wouldn't belittle him for his struggles.

"That's wonderful." She pushed past him. "Show me what you've done."

With one quick motion, he grabbed the sheaf of papers near the printer and stuffed them into a manila folder.

She pretended not to notice and focused instead on the tiny microphone and headset near the mousepad. "Ooh." She ran a finger over the slender black cord. "The system is voice-activated?"

"Uh-huh. I've been trying to work with both the fake arm and the voice software. When one frustrates me, I switch to the other."

Working his way back to normal—just like her. "When did you get all this?"

"I ordered it the night you pushed me in the snow."

He did? A thrill rippled through her, dissolving all doubt. She whirled and wrapped her hands around his waist. "I'm so proud of you!"

Surprise knocked him off-balance for a breath. But on the next inhale his arm snaked around her hips. She snuggled closer, fitting so perfectly in his embrace—even if he couldn't hold her with both arms. She tilted her head up, caught the warm glow in his eyes. Inside her rib cage, her heart melted to a puddle of goo. Every smile, every touch they'd shared had roused her attraction, drawing her to him like a moth.

He bent and touched his lips to hers. She welcomed his invasion, mouth parting under the slightest pressure. His breath, sweet and cool, melded with hers. Her arms rose as he deepened the kiss. Even through the layers of clothing he still wore, she swore she felt his heartbeat. Or perhaps she felt her own, straining to burst from her chest.

The world tilted, stealing the breath from her lungs, and she broke the contact on a sharp inhale. Her thumb lightly traced the pale scar that marred his right cheek. "Is this from the accident too?"

He stiffened and stepped out of her embrace. "Yeah," he said flatly. "The accident."

His bitterness tinged the air, turning a sweet moment into a sour memory. Her fault. She had to tread softly around what had happened to him. Eventually, she hoped, he'd understand she didn't care about his missing limb. And because she didn't care, the handicap would become less devastating to him.

"I'm sorry," she murmured. "I shouldn't have asked."

Opening the drawer to his left, he pulled out a cordovan leather–bound book embossed with the words In House Dining in gold. "Here. Choose a meal based on cuisine or restaurant. I'll just be a few minutes."

She smiled shyly. "Okay if I play with your equipment for a while?"

"Huh?"

Her fingers threaded through the voice appliance cords, dangled them near his face. "This," she said on a giggle.

"Oh. Umm . . ." His complexion paled. "I don't have internet access up here. I'm only testing this stuff on documents."

"That's fine. I want to see how it works. Maybe Richie can find it in the budget to add a few of these voice programs to Ski-Hab's occupational therapy program next year."

"There's something that confuses me. I would think companies would be lining up to get involved in a program like Ski-Hab. Yet, Mrs. Bascomb said she and her dime bag group raised the funds for some of the equipment. You said this Winter Wonderland we're going to raises money for Ski-Hab. And Kerri-Sue mentioned there's a community fund-raiser every summer. Why put the burden on the townspeople? Has Richie ever tried just approaching companies for sponsorship, rather than relying on the residents?"

"He prefers not to. Too much involvement from outside interests might compromise the program's goals." Her beliefs, not Richie's, though the entire Ski-Hab staff tended to agree. Unfortunately, lying about these details only added to her list of sins against Doug, weighing down her heart. The sooner she told him the truth, the better. In fact, she thought, as she flipped open the book of menus, she'd call for the quickest and easiest meal she could get to push the evening along.

Exhausted and sweaty, Doug craved a shower. But could he risk taking the time while Lyn played around with his laptop? Craning his neck, he took a deep whiff of his armpit. Phew. Yeah, he had to roll those dice. No way he could sit downwind from her in his current state. He raced to the bathroom, turned the showerhead on full blast, and stripped. Without waiting for the water to fully heat up, he ducked inside the shower stall and scrubbed himself clean in record time. All the while he soaped and rinsed, his mind ticked off time.

What was she looking at now? Worried that Ace would try to check up on him, he'd password-coded his article-in-progress and all his notes about Brooklyn. Thank God. Without the internet adapter, she couldn't check his recent online searches. So, really, he had nothing to worry about. Still, he finished the shower, skipped the shave, and dressed in jeans and a T-shirt. When he returned to the kitchen area, barefoot because he didn't want to waste time with socks and shoes, she still sat in front of the laptop. She'd perched the headset behind her ears, and the tiny microphone sat a whisper from her lips.

She looked up at his entrance and frowned. "There's still a few bugs in this, huh?"

"You've got that mic too close." As he pushed the microphone an inch farther away from her mouth, his fingertip brushed her soft lips.

"Oh." On a shiver, she drew back.

"Try it now." He leaned over her shoulder, inhaling the spicy scent of her skin, clothes, and hair. Cinnamon and cider. Like her inn. Warm, inviting.

"Wh-what should I say?" She'd barely uttered the words

when the cursor started typing them onto her document. "Oh, look. It's working!" Her laughter rippled down his spine like a silken ribbon. "This is amazing. I've *got* to talk to Richie about this software."

He placed his hands on her shoulders and kissed the top of her head. "*You're* amazing."

"Why do you say that?" She whirled away from the screen, and wound up nose-to-nose with him.

Surrendering to temptation, he brushed his lips across her cheek, then her mouth.

Pulling away, she shivered again, this time while a smile lit up her face. In one smooth motion, she removed the headset and dropped it on the table beside the laptop. She traced the stubble of his jaw with her fingertip. "You were about to tell me why I'm amazing," she murmured.

His eyes locked on hers. "I've never met someone so passionate about a program. Tell me about your role in Ski-Hab. You must have a pretty powerful reason to be so concerned." *Like a skeleton in your closet.*

She turned away quickly, but not before he caught the clouds in her eyes. "That's boring stuff. Let's order dinner." Her index finger drew lazy curls on his prosthetic hand. "I could really go for a burger and fries, if that's okay with you."

A burger and fries? Hardly the food of the gods and certainly not a meal known for setting a mood of give-and-take. He watched her finger on his hand and suddenly understood. She requested the pedestrian food so he might avoid the issue of using silverware with his prosthesis. How could he possibly argue with her?

"Sounds perfect."

After dinner, they called the local taxi service for a ride to the Winter Wonderland. Just as Lyn had predicted, Larry appeared at the resort ten minutes later.

"Well, well," the cabbie remarked. "You're Lyn's new 'friend,' eh? Doug, right? I took you to Winterberry's the other night. Lyn, how'd you like the meal?"

"Delicious, Larry." As Doug opened the cab's passenger

door, she flashed him a knowing smirk. "What can I say? It's a gift."

One of many she had. When Doug slid onto the black vinyl seat beside her, warm air blasted his face. The old geezer must have cranked the car's heat above eighty degrees.

Larry leaned over the front seat, his gaze locked on Lyn. "Your boyfriend there couldn't decide what to get that night. Seemed to me he fretted he wouldn't make you happy."

Doug attempted an argument, but Lyn squeezed his hand and replied, "Good thing he had you to help him out."

"Dang straight," Larry agreed. "Heard he sent you flowers the next day."

She flashed her blinding smile in Doug's direction. "Yes, that's true."

At last, Larry faced forward again and shifted the cab into drive. "What kind of flowers?"

"Red roses and purple irises."

In the rearview mirror, he flashed Doug a thumbs-up. "Nice touch. That's the mark of a true gentleman. You could do a lot worse, Lynnie."

"Gee, thanks," Doug remarked dryly.

"Actually, Larry," Lyn said, "I couldn't do much better."

"Is that a fact?" Larry asked.

"No," Doug replied.

At the very same moment, Lyn said, "Dang straight."

Doug squirmed as if a hundred fire ants suddenly crawled across his flesh. Would she think him such a hero if she knew about his ulterior motives? Doubtful.

For the rest of the ride, he preferred to stare out the window at the ski chalets, snow-covered tree branches, and storefronts they passed. He needed to regroup, reanalyze, reconsider.

"A penny for your thoughts," Lyn whispered.

Gaze still fixed out the window, he murmured, "Trust me. They're worth a lot more than that."

"So are mine." On a sigh, she leaned closer, squeezed his hand. "I'm sorry. You seem to be deep in thought, and my interrupting you could be interpreted as rude. I really don't mean to be. But the truth is . . ." She toyed with the cuff of his jacket. "I want to tell you something and—"

"Here we are!" Larry bellowed from the driver's seat. "That'll be six dollars, if you please. And even if you don't please."

The fact his passengers didn't find him quite so amusing never registered on Larry as he burst into raucous laughter.

On a sigh, Doug pulled out his billfold and removed the bills from inside. As he passed them over the seat, Larry clutched his wrist. "You be good to my girl there, you hear?"

"I'm doing my best," Doug said and slid out of the cab behind Lyn. When he turned, his jaw dropped to chest level.

Under row upon row of halogen lights, the angel arch glittered like a prismatic rainbow. At the entrance stood a locked wooden box mounted on a pike with a hand-painted sign asking for a recommended donation of five dollars per person. A line of people waited with fistfuls of five-dollar bills. He and Lyn joined the line and when their turn came up, Doug surreptitiously slipped a fifty into the slot in the box.

He had to admit the scene was even more impressive than she'd boasted. Somehow the angels' wings managed to have golden tips, and the faces were so intricately carved, they looked real enough to believe in. Up ahead, the diamond spires and turrets of a castle pierced the starlit sky. Adults and children marveled, oohing their delight as they pointed out one unique item after another, from the reindeer to the sleigh full of toys, all detailed and realistic, yet created from nothing more than frozen water.

"Isn't it beautiful?" She pulled him along with her, gaping at the glittering snowflakes, giggling at the lifelike penguins in their formal attire.

The more animated she became, the more his resolve to dig out the truth faltered. He had to get back on track before she charmed him into forgetting. And what exactly had she wanted to tell him in the cab, before loudmouth Larry ruined the moment?

At the end of the exhibit sat a dilapidated double-wide trailer covered in pale blue aluminum siding, circa 1965. A dirty plastic sign next to the frost-coated sliding window listed hot beverages and several varieties of beer for sale. Doug bought them each a hot chocolate with a whipped-cream crown. At five bucks a cup, the beverages should have been dusted with gold flakes. But he smiled, handed over the ten, and pointedly ignored the glass fishbowl with the taped cardboard sign for TIPS.

With their evening quickly coming to a close, he decided to stop tap dancing around his questions and go right for the jugular. "Where did you learn to ski?"

She never batted a lash, but took a casual sip of her chocolate before replying, "My parents. Mom and Dad had a house in the Adirondacks and we'd spend every winter vacation there from the time we were babies. Mom got us started on the bunny slopes and the easy trails when we were still toddlers. Once we were skiing the challenging stuff Mom didn't like, Dad took over. How about you?"

At last. An opening he could use. No way would he let this opportunity pass him by. "I fell in love with an Olympic skier when I was a teenager. Major league crush. Decided to take up the sport on the off chance she'd show up in West Virginia looking for a skinny, awkward sixteen-year-old ski novice with acne and braces to share slalom races and bad pizza." He exhausted his meager acting abilities on one overdramatic sigh. "She never showed up though."

She looked up at him, a dollop of whipped cream framing her upper lip. "What was her name?"

He leaned over and kissed her. Soulfully. The sweet cream danced on his tongue. Nuzzling her neck beneath her jacket collar, he murmured, "Back then, she was known as Brooklyn Raine."

He expected her to gasp, or rattle off denials, but she didn't. Instead, she drew a finger down his scarred cheek to his jawline. "So you know. Thank God."

He was the one to pull back in surprise. "You're not upset?"

"No." She flashed that blinding smile he recalled from his adolescent fantasies. "Honestly? I'm relieved. I've been trying to figure out how to tell you."

"Ace said it was a great big secret."

"It is. But you and I . . ." Her voice trailed off, and she broke eye contact to stare at the turrets of the enormous ice castle. "I can't play shy, Doug. I've never been good at head games. Not even on the circuit. The truth is I like you. A lot. And I couldn't in good conscience continue to pursue whatever the attraction is between us while holding on to a lie."

Guilt stabbed him behind the eyes. His own conscience, sounding remarkably like Ace's voice, chastised, *Tell her, idiot.*

"There she is!"

Doug turned at the outburst and froze. Flashbulbs lit up the night, reflected off the ice and fractured into prisms of blinding color. An ocean of people raced toward them.

"Brooklyn!" Someone shouted—Lorenzo Akers.

Where had *he* come from? Doug ducked inside his collar, prayed the cockroach didn't recognize him. Apparently, though, the buzz was reserved for Lyn alone, and not her companion.

"Why have you been hiding out all these years?" Akers asked.

"How do you feel about April stealing your spotlight?" a woman chimed in.

A microphone popped out of nowhere and brushed across her nose. "Will you be at your sister's wedding?"

"Can you turn this way please?" The flashing lights popped, sizzling his retinas. He blinked, but his vision remained pixellated.

"Is your mentally handicapped nephew involved in the Ski-Hab program at Mount Elsie?" Akers pestered. "Is that why they're here?"

Holy . . .

Doug couldn't even finish the swearword that came to mind. Like locusts, the crowd swarmed, buzzing with questions and jostling to get closer to their prey.

Beside him, a shivering Lyn folded in on herself, shrinking as if to hide inside his jacket pocket. The color in her cheeks had bleached away, leaving her chalk-white. Her breath came in quick spurts, close to hyperventilating. Her pupils had shrunk to pinpoints. Good God. He had to get her out of here.

"Doug!" Somewhere beyond the clamor, Ace shouted his name. "Doug!"

"Ace!" he called back. "Get us outta here."

Wrapping his real arm around Lyn's waist, he used his prosthesis to push past the first ring of screaming humanity. Someone in the crowd shoved back, and Doug tightened his grip on Lyn. God, now he knew how shark bait felt. The frenzy around them grew more physical, more violent.

Suddenly, from the outskirts of the crowd came half a dozen men brandishing brooms and hockey sticks.

"Here now!" a bald man with a round pudgy face beneath a New England Patriots knit cap exclaimed. "Get out of here, you vultures!"

"Let them through!" Another man, this one short and thin and wearing a black hunting cap, shouted as he held a hockey stick like a guardrail, dividing the crowd down the middle.

Doug continued to elbow and shoulder his way through the throng, but the bizarrely armed force of men gave him a wider berth to use. At last he spotted Ace and dragged Lyn in a straight line to him.

"What's going on?" he demanded as he reached Ace's side. "Where did all these people come from?"

"My fault," Ace said with a grimace. "Come on. Let's get to the car and I'll explain everything."

Chapter Eighteen

Once they'd reached Ace's Escalade, Doug yanked open the back door and shoved Lyn inside, then slid in beside her. Shuddering and ghostly pale, she huddled against him.

Ace got behind the wheel and started the engine. "Where to?"

"Home," Lyn said through chattering teeth. "Take me home. Please."

"Umm . . ." Over the black leather headrest, Ace flashed an uncertain glance at Doug. "I don't think that's such a hot idea."

The headlights shone on the crowd surging toward them, flesh-eating zombies from some B horror movie.

Doug stifled his own shudders as Ace turned around again. "Why don't you tell us what's going on? Who are all those people?"

"Reporters, mostly. A few rabid fans." Ace's worried face reflected in the rearview mirror. "They know."

"Who knows?" Doug pressed. "Knows what?"

"Me," Lyn murmured into his chest. "They know about me. Who I am. Or was." She drew in a sharp breath. "Or am. I guess."

Doug's heart sank. Yeah, he'd figured as much when they started screaming questions and calling her Brooklyn. But he'd kinda hoped they were there because Lyn won the Publishers Clearing House sweepstakes. "How exactly did this happen?"

"My fault," Ace said again.

Great. The story of a lifetime had just slipped away like a greased eel. He'd been *thisclose* to not only rejuvenating his career, but reintroducing the sports world to an amazing woman.

Until Ace blew those plans to dust. Doug recalled all the arguments and debates about the article he planned to write. Had Ace orchestrated this disaster intentionally?

Thump! A hand slammed against the window, and Lyn screamed. Curling into a tight ball, she cradled her head in her folded arms and murmured, "I hate this, I hate this, I hate this, I hate this."

"I don't care where we go, just get us outta here," Doug growled as he pulled the shivering Lyn against him.

"Richie's," Lyn said from inside Doug's jacket. "Take me to Richie's."

"That," Ace replied, "I can do."

Sounding the horn in short blasts, he drove slowly away from the grasping hands and rapid-fire questions. Once they reached the open road, he hit the gas and barreled toward the highway.

Doug kept his real arm around Lyn while his prosthetic hand gripped the door handle to keep from crushing her on the road's curves. Under normal circumstances, he'd pause to marvel at his prosthesis' almost instinctive motions yet again. But in the wake of disaster, a little finger curl barely registered on the Oh-My-God scale. "Okay, Ace, what's going on? What was all that about? What happened? How'd they find out?"

"Someone recognized Becky."

"Becky?" Lyn sat up. "My niece?"

"Yeah. My fault. I totally admit it."

Lyn sighed, the sound of an exasperated parent with a disobedient child. "You couldn't just leave her alone, could you?"

"Look, I'm sorry, okay? Becky and I hit it off. I mean, I really like her. She's funny, smart, and not bowled over by all the fan frenzy. So we spent the last few days together. But you know how it gets when I'm here."

"You mean, when you draw attention to yourself?" Lyn retorted.

Right hand upraised, he turned in the seat to face her. "I swear. If I'd known who she was, I wouldn't have drawn so much attention to us. Nobody told me she was anything more than your niece."

The Escalade drifted out of the left lane, into the center. From behind them, a car horn blared.

"Turn around and drive!" Lyn exclaimed.

"Whoa!" Ace faced the road again, both hands on the steering wheel as he muttered, "Sorry. You know, now that I think about it, that's probably why she wasn't impressed with the crowds around me. She's used to it from that television show with her mom and Jeff—"

"Oh, for God's sake, Ace, shut up!" Lyn snapped. "This isn't about *you.*"

Doug cupped her hand in his. "Easy, sweetheart."

With a deep breath, her tone calmed. "I have to think. What happened next, Ace? Don't look at me. Keep your eyes on the road and just tell me."

Ace shrugged. "Next thing I know, your sister shows up at the base lodge with that Jeff guy. The crowds are going nuts, and Michael starts to freak."

"Oh God, Michael." Gripping the headrest, she leaned forward. "Is he okay?"

"Yeah," Ace replied. "April got him calmed down, but not before he said the name 'Aunt Brooklyn' in front of Lorenzo Akers. Old Buzzard Beak put it together instantly."

Doug sucked in a breath. Poor kid. Even in the dim light of the parlor the other night, he'd noted the telltale eyes of a child with Down syndrome. If the crowd at the lodge was anything close to what they'd just experienced at Winter Wonderland, Michael had every right to freak.

"Oh God," Lyn repeated, this time with a groan.

"Three hours later," Ace went on, "a hundred reporters are in town, all looking for the Raine sisters."

The groaning grew into a keening wail.

In an attempt to placate her, Doug squeezed her fingers with gentle pressure. "I'm sure Michael didn't mean for this to happen."

She yanked away as if his hand were on fire and curled up against the SUV's passenger door. "Of course he didn't mean it. I'm not blaming him. I don't even blame April, though I warned her she shouldn't come here with so much media attention focused on her and Jeff." Once again, she turned her attention to Ace. "Are they okay? April, Jeff, and the kids?"

"Headed back home. Slipped out with some help from Mrs. Bascomb and her son."

"Well, thank God for that, at least," she said with a sigh.

"But there are reporters camped outside Mount Elsie, outside your inn, and all over the village. It's a free-for-all."

She covered her face with her hands and rocked. "I need to think. I can't think. I don't know what to do. Richie will know. Just get me to Richie's. I can't think."

Doug refused to simply sit and watch her fall apart before his eyes. Particularly since he didn't understand what had set her off in the first place. "Wait. I don't get it. What's the big deal? I mean, yeah, I admit that whole scene in the Winter Wonderland was a little intense. But nothing you can't handle, right? Come on. You were a media darling for years. You're used to this. You know how it goes. By next week, there'll be a new story, new players, and the press will flock to some other spot."

She flashed him poisonous eyes, meant to drop him into an open grave on his next breath.

"What?" Squirming away from her lethal gaze, he leaned toward the front seat. At least the sane ones were still in the majority here. "Tell her, Ace. You know what I'm talking about. This is just a speed bump. Or in your case, I guess, a mogul run. Tell her how you do it. If anyone knows how to handle the press, it's you. You've usually got the media eating out of your hand."

Ace jammed on the brakes. The tires squealed. The rear end fishtailed as he swerved the vehicle to the shoulder of the highway. Doug's right arm collided with the tinted passenger window. If that side of his body had been flesh instead of a lifelike polymer, he might have wound up with a sleeve of bruises or a possible hairline fracture. But he felt nothing except a slight jarring.

Wasn't he the lucky guy?

In the driver's seat, Ace shifted the gear in the center console into park. Wrapping an arm around the headrest, he thrust his head into the backseat. "The price of fame, right? Suck it up and deal. That's what you think, isn't it, Doug?"

"That's what everybody thinks, Ace," he replied. "And it's not like you have it so bad. You've got money, fame, all the girls you want falling at your feet. Even the reporters fall at your feet. Only Akers hates you, and that's because you broke his nose in that scuffle at JFK."

"Yeah, right." Ace's eyes narrowed to dashes in his suddenly florid face. "And thanks to that scuffle, I've gotta bend and scrape to every peon with a camera or microphone so my butt doesn't wind up in jail again. Some yahoo asks me about my mom's breast cancer treatments or if I'd been drinking the night before I wiped out at Aspen, and I have to smile and entertain the crowds like an idiotic court jester. And as much as all that sucks wind, women celebrities have it ten times worse. Every extra pound, every bad hair day, every man they're seen with is cause for speculation and an excuse to splash photos all over television and magazines. So don't sit back there and tell me how to 'handle' my fame. Because you don't know squat, dude."

Lyn smiled grimly. "Well done, Ace. Thank you."

Ace set the Escalade in drive again. "It needed to be said."

"I meant for breaking Lorenzo Akers' nose. I don't think I ever properly thanked you for that."

"Oh, hey, no charge." He swerved to grin over his shoulder, index and middle fingers forming the international victory symbol. "Score one for us, eh?"

Lyn's shaky laughter pierced the air. When Ace added his own goofy chuckles, Doug became the minority in their trio. The only sane one.

When they pulled up in the circular driveway of Richie's A-frame cedar chalet, fat, wet snowflakes were falling from cloudy skies. Amber light glowed in the three-story triangular windows. Warmth seeped into Lyn's chilled flesh. Next to Snowed Inn, the Armstrong house represented her only sanctuary in the whole state.

Sure enough, she'd barely stepped out of the SUV when the chalet's front door opened. Phyllis Armstrong, clad in gray sweats, with her bottle-black hair wrapped in pink foam rollers, appeared on the stoop. "Hurry." She waved a hand above her lumpy hair. "Richie's in the den with the television on, monitoring the situation."

"How bad?" Lyn asked.

Even in the dark night, Lyn saw Phyllis hesitate. "Umm . . . I'll let Richie tell you."

That bad, huh? She started forward, but her legs shook so violently, she stumbled on the edge of a mound of shoveled snow. Doug wrapped his arm around her, a stabilizing force that kept her upright. Clinging to his support, she offered a drained but grateful nod. "Thank you."

She didn't fault him for what he'd said on the ride here. Well, not entirely. Those who had never lived under the microscope couldn't truly understand the enormous burden the world's eyes created. They saw the money, the glamour, and found the idea exciting. They never saw the downside: the loss of freedom, the invasion of privacy.

Marc's last photo, his cancer-ravaged face against a pristine satin pillow, popped into her head. Lorenzo Akers. Buzzard Beak, as Ace so aptly nicknamed him, had somehow managed to either bribe or slink his way into the funeral parlor outside the standard visiting hours. Alone with Marc's body for God knew how long, Akers had snapped photo after vile photo, then splashed his ill-gotten booty all over the print media. The next day, before she said her final good-bye to her husband, she saw the horrible image of Marc in his casket on the front page of her morning paper. Add that offense to the pictures Akers had printed of her leaving her father's funeral a few months earlier, and Lyn had plenty of reason to despise the members of the Fourth Estate.

She shuddered.

Doug must have misinterpreted the reason behind her reaction, because he pulled her closer and ran his hand briskly down her arm. "Come on." He hustled her over the slate stepping stone walkway. "Let's get you inside and warmed up."

Her brain still firmly lodged on the heartless Akers, she nodded.

"Looks like they were waiting for you," Ace remarked from behind them.

"Plan B," she murmured. "Plan A if they accost me at the mountain; Plan B for anywhere else in town."

"Covered all your bases, huh?" Doug asked.

"Had to." She reached the series of hand-hewn wooden stairs and the matching railing, but Phyllis didn't wait any longer.

With a shriek of "Oh, my poor girl!" the older woman swooped down, arms spread wide like a giant pink-and-black-plumed mother hen. Pulling her away from Doug, Phyllis enveloped Lyn in a fierce hug. "It's all right, Lynnie. It's going to be okay."

Beneath Phyllis' viselike embrace, Lyn allowed herself to believe the comforting words. She even managed to climb the stairs and step inside the house. Ace and Doug followed behind.

A roaring fire crackled in the living room's stone hearth. While Ace introduced Doug to Phyllis, Lyn stepped closer to the blaze, hoping to pull the chill from her bones.

On the mantel, a dozen framed photographs smiled at her: Richie and Phyllis at their daughter's wedding a few years ago, Richie and Phyllis with their first grandchild last Christmas, Richie and Phyllis with the whole family on a summer outing, Richie and Phyllis at a VFW dinner party. Always together. Richie and Phyllis.

Loneliness pinched her heart.

"Lyn?" Richie called from another room. "Is that you?"

"Of course it's Lyn," Phyllis said with an exaggerated edge. "I told you I saw the car pull up."

"You didn't drive, did you, Lyn?" Richie asked.

"No," she said, turning away from the wall of family togetherness. "Ace drove."

"There ya go, Phyllis," Richie retorted. "You had no way of knowing if the car that pulled into the driveway was Lyn's or a bunch of those bloodsucking vampires from the press. I told you not to go running out there till you knew for sure."

Phyllis shot her hands to her hips. "But it *was* her. So no harm done." Under her breath, she added, "Stubborn old coot." She nudged Lyn forward. "Go on, sweetie. He's gonna wanna see for himself that you're okay."

Okay? Hardly. Breathing, sure. Heart beating? Yeah. A little too fast, but yeah. Still, she was miles away from the clinical definition of "okay." And she didn't think she had the energy to walk across the house under her own waning power.

"Lyn?" Doug's voice whispered in her ear. "You need help?"

She barely nodded, but somehow, he knew. He always seemed to know. Taking her elbow, he led her forward at a slow, easy pace. "Where to?"

"Straight back," she murmured. "It's a sunken den, but there's a ramp from the dining room."

They walked together past the dining room with its knotty pine furnishings and the overhead light fixture made of deer antlers. Lyn averted her eyes from the wall filled with a dozen more family photographs, the timeline of a couple happily married for more than three decades. At last they descended the short ramp and stopped in a room filled with deep blue modular furniture. The far wall, covered by a ginormous television and surround system, commanded the attention of the room's lone occupant.

"Richie?" Lyn asked.

The steely-haired man in the wheelchair turned, eyes narrowed with tender concern. "Ah, sweetheart, are you okay?" His gaze swept over Doug. "Sawyer. Didn't expect you here."

"We were together when the press accosted us," she replied.

Beside her, Doug stiffened. Why? She turned to look at him and noticed how his eyes narrowed in Richie's direction. A minute or two passed, but then realization woke in her brain. "You didn't know Richie was an amputee, did you?"

"Doug's only seen me with my stems," Richie replied and rolled himself closer. "Isn't that right?"

On a quick exhale, Doug's posture relaxed. "Yes, sir. Excuse me for asking, but I'm just curious. Were you the first Ski-Hab student?"

Richie laughed. "Nah. I lost my legs a long time before Ski-

Hab. But I participated in a ski rehab program in Europe years ago. Brought the idea back here. Lyn had wanted to do something to honor her husband's memory, and Ski-Hab was the result." He picked up a remote control and beckoned Lyn closer with a crooked finger. "Now, let's get to the problem at hand. I've been recording the news reports. Take off your coats, have a seat, and we'll see what we've got."

Lyn managed to make it to the bolstered sofa under her own steam, but she left her coat zipped around her. Regardless of the heat in the house, her shivers hadn't completely disappeared. When she sank onto the cushions, Doug sat beside her and cupped her hand. Heat sizzled from his fingertips to hers. Either he had a fever, or she was more chilled than she thought.

"Hey, Richie," Ace said as he loped into the room. "How's it rolling?"

"All uphill," Richie retorted.

Ace grinned. "I hear that." He plopped down on the sofa next to Lyn, sandwiching her.

Ordinarily, she'd shove him away, but right now, with her dam walls about to crumble, she'd take all the shoring up she could get.

"Everybody ready?" Richie held the remote above his head, pointed toward the massive screen.

One shaky breath first, then Lyn said, "Go."

Richie had recorded at least a dozen different news reports from various television stations, both local and national. Every one of them ran with the same angle: "Did you know that April Raine of *Taking Sides* fame has an equally famous sister?"

Videos flashed in a blur. Brooklyn Raine accepting her gold medal at the Winter Olympics. Brooklyn Raine crossing the finish line in record time at the World Cup. Brooklyn Raine and Marc Cheviot waving from a Matterhorn float at the Disney World Electric Parade. Brooklyn Raine, swathed in white tulle, and Marc Cheviot in a white tuxedo, beaming at each other outside St. Patrick's Cathedral. Brooklyn Raine walking out of the funeral parlor where her father's services were held. Brooklyn Raine walking out of another funeral parlor where her husband's services were held. And finally, Brooklyn Raine walking hand-in-hand with Doug outside the Winter Wonderland ice sculpture park. On that last scene, the screen split with Doug and Lyn smiling at each other on the left. Meanwhile, a clip of April, Jeff, and the kids pushing their way out of a crowd at the base lodge of Mount Elsie popped up on the right.

Whatever the talking heads said didn't register, couldn't compete with the high-pitched buzz in her ears. Nausea roiled her stomach. Her skin hardened to battle armor, cold and steely.

At last, the torture ended. But, based on the grim faces around her, Lyn knew the nightmare had only begun.

Richie spoke first. "We gotta get you outta here, sweetheart. Someplace where they can't find you."

She looked from one stern expression to the other. No one gainsaid Richie's suggestion. "I-I could go to Summer's—"

"The last place you can go is to family," Richie shot back. "If the press has copped to you and April being related, Summer will be next. You want that?"

God, no. Lyn sighed. Poor Summer. Already, her marriage showed cracks. How much of the paparazzi microscope would it take to completely destroy whatever wedded bliss she and Brad still clung to?

"She can come home with me," Doug said.

She swerved to face him, certain she'd see a huge leer or smirk, a hint he joked with her. But his expression looked solemn. Steady. Completely serious.

"No." The denial came from both Richie and Ace simultaneously.

"Why not?" Doug demanded. "Completely on the up-and-up here, guys. My place is big, secure, and anonymous. She'd have her own bedroom, twenty-four-hour security, and the ability to stay in contact with anyone she wants to while still maintaining a low profile."

Lyn's steely armor softened. Beside her sat a white knight, a man who cared enough to *care*. Unlike these other two Neanderthals.

"Actually," she said, "that's not a bad idea. New York is the perfect place for me to hide in plain sight. No one knows

Doug. Even if the press eventually finds out who he is, there'd be nothing to link him to me."

"Actually," Ace replied, his tone more frigid than dry ice, "a lot of people know Doug. A lot of press people. And there'd be an awful lot to link him to you because of what he does for a living."

She shook her head. "Why? Because he works for you? It would still be too great a stretch for anyone to link you with me and by extension, Doug with me."

"Is that what he told you?" Ace glared at Doug. "That he works for me?"

"No." Doug eased his arm away from her. A subtle signal, but the gesture put Lyn on alert. "I never said that."

Her brow furrowed as she studied Doug, confusion buzzing in her brain. "Of course you did. I asked how you knew Ace."

"And I said that I'd known Ace since his first professional competition. That I was, sort of, in promotion."

"Right. So?"

The room grew eerily silent, with three pairs of eyes looking everywhere but at her. Cold sweat broke out on her arms.

Sort of. He'd said sort of. "What exactly am I missing?"

Doug ducked his head, sighed. "I work—that is, I *used to work*—for *The Sportsman.*"

"*The Sportsman*," she repeated. *The Sportsman* magazine. She doubted he handled their marketing. Her heart crept into her throat. "You're a . . ." The word stuck, refusing to leave her lips.

Please, God, please don't let it be true. Don't let me be more of an idiot than I feel right now.

But apparently, God wasn't taking requests today.

"I'm a reporter, Lyn."

"And your arm? I'm guessing you didn't lose your arm in some drunken car accident."

Something about the nap of the couch cushion fascinated Doug all of a sudden because he kept his gaze fixed there. "I lost my arm in Iraq. I was embedded with Giles Markham's army unit. I'm the only survivor of a Humvee explosion."

"So, all this time, you've been spying on me? Taking notes? Planning to write a story about me?"

He didn't answer, still couldn't look her in the eye, and she had her confirmation. But she noted the same guilty expressions worn by Ace and Richie. The fine hairs danced on her nape.

"You knew, didn't you? Both of you."

Richie held out his hands in supplication. "Now, Lynnie, honey, it's not what you think. Doug really did need our help, and I had no way of knowing you and he would even meet, much less become involved with one another. When Kerri-Sue told me, I—"

"Kerri-Sue knew too?" She bit back a groan. Just how widespread did this conspiracy reach?

"Not at first," Doug interjected. "She Googled me, found out the truth."

Ha. Google. Why hadn't Lyn thought of that? Oh, maybe because she never thought her friends would deceive her so horribly.

"Kerri-Sue trusted that Richie wouldn't have accepted me into the program if I meant you any harm," Doug continued. "And I don't, Lyn. Really. In fact, now that you know the truth, we can make this work in your favor. All you have to do is give me an exclusive interview. I'll get the press off your back—"

Despite legs more wobbly than Jell-O, she got to her feet, pointed toward the doorway. "Get out." Her volume stayed low, but the tone was pure white-hot rage. "You and Ace, get out of here."

Doug rose and walked toward her with slow, deliberate steps, as if he approached a raving lunatic. "Now, Lyn, please. It's not what it seems."

"No?" She tossed back her head and laughed bitterly. "Oh, well, thank God for that. Because it *seems* like my friends are conspiring with my enemy. It *seems* like I've been lied to and set up and made a fool of by people I've trusted for years. So by all means, Doug, tell me I'm wrong."

Even if he had attempted to take her up on that request, she refused to remain in this house one moment longer. Hands curled into tight fists, she turned away from the monsters surrounding her. "On second thought, you guys stay. I'm out of here. Phyllis?" she called as she strode from the den. "Would you call Larry and have him pick me up ASAP? I'll wait for him outside."

Chapter Nineteen

Ignoring the cacophony of arguments from the men inside the Armstrong house, Lyn waited outside in the wet snowfall. She didn't care if she resembled Frosty the Snowman. Cold didn't bother her anymore. Her fury kept her toasty warm.

How could they treat her so badly? Ace, she supposed, simply didn't understand her aversion to the spotlight he so obviously adored. Doug, no doubt, saw her only as a story. But Richie? Richie, who knew and understood the pain she'd endured when Akers printed that photo? Richie had gone behind her back to put her in the direct line of fire. And his duplicity cut past her ribs, tearing her heart to shreds.

By the time Larry's familiar, battered blue Chevy pulled into the driveway, she'd grown numb. Numb from the frigid night air, numb from the agony of betrayal. Without waiting for Larry to get out of the car to help, she yanked open the passenger door and slid inside.

"Where we headed, sweetheart?"

Where, indeed. She had no idea. For the moment, she said, "Just drive, Larry. Please."

"You got it."

He pulled out of the driveway and headed back toward the center of town. For a while, the only sound in the car came from the occasional static of the dispatch service and the squeal of the windshield wipers clearing the fallen snowflakes.

"Saw what happened on the news," he said at last.

Great. She rubbed her temples with icy fingertips. "Please, Larry. I can't talk about it right now."

"Whatever you want, Lyn," he said. "I just want you to know that you need anything, anything at all, you ask, okay?" Staring out at the endless black highway, she murmured, "Okay. Thanks."

She finally made him drop her off at Winterberry Café, where she begged to use the phone in the owner's office. When April answered her cell, the dam inside her burst, and she broke down.

"Oh, thank God!" April exclaimed. "Where have you been? Are you okay?"

"No," she said. She wanted to tell her sister everything. About Ace. And Doug. And Richie. But any words she tried to utter wound up choked by tears or unintelligible thanks to the shudders racking her.

"Okay, okay. Breathe, sweetie," April soothed. "Where are you?"

"Winterberry's."

"Not out in the open!" April stated with surprise.

"No." But she looked around the cramped room filled with restaurant supplies and invoices anyway, to be sure she was alone. "I'm in the office."

"Okay, can you stay there?"

"Uh-huh."

"Give me a number to reach you."

Lyn managed to rattle off the phone number.

"Sit tight and give me five minutes. Mrs. B.'s waiting to hear from you. She's got your bag packed and Aaron's car gassed up and ready. Stay where you are until you hear back from me."

Once April hung up, Lyn sank into the squeaky chair, placed her head on the desk, and wrapped her arms around her ears. Still, the recriminations screamed inside her brain.

Way to go, Lyn. Of all the men for you to fall for, you chose a reporter? Now what?

Because you fell hard, kiddo. And he just shattered your heart.

How would she ever recover?

The restaurant's office phone rang, and she hesitantly picked up. "Thank you for calling Winterberry's. How may I direct your call?"

"Got a pen?" April asked.

Assured Lyn was ready, April gave her a series of directions and summed up with, "Aaron's on his way to Winterberry's with the car. Once you're on the road, don't stop till you're way out of town. If you have to go to the bathroom, go now or hold it for the next three hours."

Lyn stared at the chicken scratch she'd hastily written on a blank invoice sheet. "What exactly is this place?"

"It's the perfect hiding place. The house belongs to a client of Rainey-Day-Wife. He's away in Brussels on business until after the New Year. Take care of his dog, his houseplants, and his python, and the place is yours till he comes home."

Lyn swallowed hard. "His python?"

"It's in an aquarium in a locked room. You don't have to do anything more than feed it one mouse every week or so and make sure the water dish is full. All the instructions are taped to the outside of the tank. It's a piece of cake, really."

A python? She shivered. *Ick.*

But then again, honestly, what was the difference between a caged python or the nest of vipers she'd just left? At least the python didn't try to be anything but a python.

"And what kind of dog?" If April mentioned any breed with a remotely aggressive reputation, she'd have to rethink this whole get-out-of-Dodge plan. Larry had offered his couch for her to crash on. A crazy idea that was beginning to sound like a reasonable alternative.

"Greyhound. A rescue dog. Sleek and sweet. Her name is Ginger and she's an absolute doll. She just needs to be exercised a lot. You okay to keep up with her?"

"To have a safe place to hide, I'd run a three-minute mile right now."

April laughed. "Good girl. Okay, the front door has a combination lock, so write the numbers down and keep all this info someplace safe. Ready?"

"Ready." Quickly, she jotted down the combination. "Got it."

"Don't call me again, because we don't want to tip anyone

off to where you are. Once you get to the house, make yourself at home. Tomorrow morning, call Brenda at the office. Tell her you're Mrs. Snow and you wanted to thank her for the service our company provided. That way I'll know you're there and safe. Good with that?"

"Uh-huh."

"If you need anything at all, call Brenda as Mrs. Snow. She'll get the message to me. Okay?"

"Okay." She gripped the receiver tighter and whispered, "April? Thanks. I owe you."

"No, you don't. It's my fault you're being hounded right now. You warned me this might happen. I didn't listen, and I'm sorry."

"It's okay. Really. It'll all be okay."

But only if her heart could repair itself.

The sanctuary April had arranged sat in a gated community, completely secure and miles from anyone she knew. Apparently April had taken care of all the details, because when Lyn pulled up outside the guard's house in Aaron Bascomb's car, ready to stutter out some lame excuse about visiting a friend, the man simply tipped his cap and held out a cardboard tag.

"Good evening, Mrs. Snow. This is your parking permit. Please make sure it's hanging from your rearview mirror at all times, as our security patrol does random checks throughout the neighborhood day and night. The house you're looking for is twenty-three Clay Court. Follow this road to the first stop sign, make a left, then a quick right. The house will be directly facing you in the center of the circle. Red door with a big white sparkly Christmas wreath."

She took the parking permit and offered him a tired smile. "Thank you . . . ?" She paused. Despite the halogen lights from the guardhouse behind him, she couldn't read the name printed on his badge in the darkness of night.

"George," he supplied. "I wish you a pleasant stay with us, Mrs. Snow. If we can be of service to you while you're here, please let us know. You can reach us twenty-four hours a day by dialing nine-zero on your house phone."

"Thank you, George." Rolling up the window, she drove

through the raised gate and followed the road to the first stop sign as directed. Hours after midnight, the neighborhood of cookie-cutter townhouses on the fringe of an eighteen-hole golf course slumbered under cloudy skies. She spotted the door with its glittery wreath easily and pulled into the short driveway, then put the car in park and turned off the engine. With her purse in hand, she grabbed her emergency suitcase from the backseat and hurried to the front door.

When she punched in the door code, the locks clicked, and she slipped inside. On the left wall beside the door, as promised, she found the light switch and flipped it up. Instantly the house burst into illuminated life, but exhaustion finally claimed Lyn, leaving her too drained to check out her surroundings. She dropped her bags on the floor, then slumped against the wall. Sliding to a squatting position, she covered her face with her hands.

The *click-click* of toenails on terra-cotta tile caused her to look up. A giant dog raced toward her, its whiplike tail wagging furiously. Thank God April had warned her that Ginger was friendly and eager to please. She hadn't mentioned how adorable the dog was with her long nose, bright eyes, and mouth almost shaped like she smiled in welcome.

"So you're my new roommate," she said with a sigh.

The brown and white dog swiped a cold, wet nose over her cheek, which, to her surprise, was just the cure for her moment of self-pity. Renewed, she stood, threw her shoulders back, and inhaled deeply to give her spirits a lift.

"How about you give me Le Grande Tour?" she said as she scratched her new best friend's head.

After double-checking that she'd locked the front door, she strode through the house, Ginger as her escort. First stop, the kitchen, where she found glass cabinetry, marble countertops, and stainless steel appliances. On the center butcher block sat a frosted glass vase filled with red and white roses and evergreen branches. Instantly, her mind kicked back to the flowers Doug had sent her after their first date.

How long had he planned to string her along with dinners and flowers? And once he'd reeled her in enough to get the story he wanted, how quickly would he have skipped town? Certainly before any other reporters learned what he knew. *Joke's on you, Doug. Ace's foolish interest in Becky totally screwed up your plan to be the one who revealed my true identity in the public arena.* When exactly had he known who she really was? Had Ace confided her secret, and Doug had purposely used his injury to get accepted into Ski-Hab in the hopes of getting close to her? Maybe the prosthesis was a fake. Could he have pretended to be an amputee, all the while hiding a fully functioning arm inside his clothes?

She snorted. *Get a grip, babe. No man would chop off a limb just to find out about you.*

God, she was so tired. Her brain couldn't play these games any longer.

Averting her eyes from the roses and all they represented, she picked up the notepad beside the vase.

Welcome to The Links was written in precise script. *I stocked the kitchen for you so you'll find basic staples, prepared meals, and cleaning supplies. If you need anything else, there's a prepaid cell phone on the dining room table. My name and number are already programmed in.*

Think of yourself as part of a witness protection program. Use nothing that can identify you. No bank cards or checks. Pay any expenses with cash only. If you run low on funds, call me. April's taking care of all your finances until this is over. And she said to tell you, "You bet your curvy butt you'll pay me back."

That comment, so perfectly April, drew a smile from Lyn when she needed it most.

The letter continued, detailing names and directions to stores in the area, delivery services for everything from dry cleaning to pizza, and emergency contact information. As she read through the pages and finally reached Brenda's signature, her eyelids grew heavier and she began to yawn.

"Well, Ginger, my girl," she told the greyhound. "I think it's time for us to call it a night. We'll have plenty of time to get acquainted tomorrow. How about you show me to my room?"

Chapter Twenty

The following morning when Lyn went downstairs for breakfast, she found the kitchen stocked with everything that Brenda had promised in her note, and more. Coffee, half-and-half, fresh fruit, and all her favorite low-carb foods. Only one person knew enough about her habits to mastermind this mini-miracle.

Thank you, April.

Ginger, who'd spent the night on a large sheepskin pet mattress at the foot of Lyn's bed, nudged her hand, then sprinted for the door.

"Okay, girl." She reached for the folded bit of paper with the door combination, tucked it into her jeans pocket, and headed for the foyer's utility closet. Sure enough, the dog's leash hung on a hook within easy reach. Lyn also noticed the unit's washer/dryer combo, detergent, fabric softener, dryer sheets, a broom and dustpan, and a box of tall kitchen garbage bags. Her organized little heart went pitter-pat.

The townhouse's owner, Michael Berman, was a veterinarian, divorced, with two school-age daughters and a passion for greyhound rescue. Judging by the photos she'd seen in the family room, he was a fairly good-looking guy. Since he'd opened his home to her no questions asked, she surmised he was also generous and compassionate. So why couldn't she have fallen for Michael Berman, DVM, instead of Douglas Sawyer, RAT?

Don't go there, she scolded herself.

Yeah, sure. Great advice. Too bad her heart refused to listen. At least a thousand times over the last twelve hours, she'd relived that one magic moment underneath the ice angel wings. Doug had leaned close to her, his warm breath caressing the scrap of her neck between her scarf and her jacket collar. He'd told her about his teenage crush, let her know that he knew she was really Brooklyn Raine, and before she could make any excuses, he'd kissed her. And for that one perfect instant, she'd known bliss.

Aaaargh! Enough! She had to stop daydreaming and get on with life AD: after Doug.

Ginger concurred by scraping a paw over the steel front door.

"Okay, okay," Lyn told the impatient greyhound as she grabbed the leash. "Let's go for a walk, sweetie."

She slipped into her jacket, then clamped the leash to Ginger's collar. The dog did the rest. With a quick yank, Ginger dragged Lyn out the door and into a sunny, crisp December day. Even if Lyn wanted to check out the scenery or meet any neighbors who strolled by on their way to the golf course, the greyhound had other plans.

Ginger pulled her in a perfect circle around the outskirts of the community at a runner's pace. When they passed the guard's station where she'd arrived last night, a different man in uniform bobbed his flat cap. "Morning, Mrs. Snow. I see Ginger's in high spirits today."

"I guess so," Lyn managed to say through exhausted panting. She didn't even blink at his use of her alias. Apparently, April had covered all the bases for her. And Lyn had tried to lecture her about handling the media? No wonder she and Jeff had looked at Lyn like she'd suddenly sprouted snakes for hair that night. April not only knew how to keep the press at bay, she'd also come up with an amazing contingency plan to keep Lyn safe and hidden.

Ginger tugged again, nearly upending Lyn. She stumbled, slamming her toe against the curb. "Is she always like this?"

"She's a greyhound, ma'am." The guard shrugged as if that enigmatic reply covered a multitude of explanations.

Maybe it did. Lyn knew next to nothing about greyhounds.

"So she is," Lyn said to the guard, just before Ginger hurried her out of earshot.

Twenty minutes later, they were back in front of the red door with the white wreath. Ginger galloped up the two cement steps and sat, waiting, while Lyn fumbled with the paper in her pocket and tried to catch her breath.

"The least you could do is pant," she grumbled at the dog.

But Ginger simply stared with those soft, melted chocolate eyes and flashed that greyhound grin.

Shaking her head, Lyn punched in the code and opened the front door. A digital version of Beethoven's *Fifth Symphony* emitted from the kitchen.

The cell phone! Dagnabbit. She'd forgotten to call Brenda this morning. She unclipped the leash from Ginger's collar, then expended her last spurt of adrenaline in a race to the butcher block, where she'd left the stupid phone.

She lunged, pushed the ON button, and placed the phone to her ear. "Hello?"

"Lyn?" a voice full of concern said. "It's Brenda. Are you all right?"

She let out a long breath. "Yes. I'm sorry. I completely forgot to call you this morning."

"You sound out of breath. What's wrong?"

Explaining would take too long and take too much out of her. So she opted for the one-word reply. "Ginger."

Brenda laughed. "Oh, right. She's a huge ball of energy, isn't she? Cute as can be, though, and a real love. Everything's okay with you then?"

"As okay as it can be."

"You're sure?"

"Yes." Her pounding heart rocketed up her throat. "Why? Have you heard something?"

"No," Brenda replied. "All's quiet on the western front, which bothers me more than when there's a buzz. But that's just the mom in me, looking for chaos in the heart of calm. So for now, sit tight. If there's news, I'll be in touch. Go relax and catch your breath. If you need anything, call me."

Brenda hung up, and Lyn placed the phone back on the counter. Ginger, all smiles and wagging tail, looked up adoringly at her.

Now what? An endless day stretched before her with nothing to do but think. A dangerous pastime.

For three days, Lyn managed to pass hours with Ginger, an endless stream of idiotic television shows, and the occasional peek-and-run with Monty the Python. As day turned to night, night to day, and back again, Lyn had a fairly good idea how a prisoner felt in solitary confinement.

But by day four, her mind could no longer avoid reliving her last few hours at home. How an evening of fun and laughter had become a hurried escape from all that she held dear. At first, she fought against her pitching emotions with banal distractions. In the family room, she pulled out a photo album. Curled up on the couch, she flipped through pictures of Dr. Berman and his kids. Two pretty dark-haired girls with pixie faces and matching pink bikinis squeezed the stuffing out of Dad at a water park. The same two girls cuddled with him in an enormous rope hammock on a white sandy beach. Another snapshot had the trio huddled around a birthday cake in the townhouse's kitchen, half a dozen candles glowing in the twilit room. Page after page of happy memories, of precious family moments. Just like Richie and Phyllis.

The one thrill Lyn would never know: a family of her own. She glanced down at the glossy images again and traced a finger over Dr. Berman's indulgent smile. Doug would have made a wonderful father.

No. Not Doug.

Actually, yes. Doug. Or, at least, the Doug she'd built up in her heart. Unfortunately, the real man fell far too short of her fantasy version.

By afternoon, the tears finally started. And refused to stop. Ginger tried to help with a nudge here and a lick there. But being a dog, she really had little or no opinion on the perfidy of human men. Lyn needed more than a cold, wet nose and a run around the neighborhood. She needed reasons, an explanation, an apology. No more accusations or excuses. Just some straight dirt.

Before she could talk herself out of it, she headed for the kitchen. Cell phone in hand, she dialed a phone number as familiar to her as her own at Snowed Inn.

Richie picked up on the second ring. "Hello?"

"Richie?" she rasped through a throat scraped raw from excessive tears.

"Lyn? Where are you? Are you okay?"

Despite a sudden quake in her knees, she remained standing in the hope that a stiffer posture would make her sound more forceful, more in control. "I'm not telling you where I am, and I'm not okay. I need an explanation from you, Rich."

"Aw, come on, Lynnie. You know me. Come home and we'll talk."

"No. Talk now. From the hip, Richie."

"Where do you want me to start?"

"Start with your selection process. Why Doug Sawyer?"

"Because he's a decent guy who needed our help. Ace Riordan vouched for him, and I reviewed his medical records as well as his personal info. He was a perfect candidate on a multitude of levels. He was in decent physical shape, with ski experience prior to his amputation. And even though he's technically a civilian, he sustained his injuries in combat. You wanted to start taking on civilians, and I set the plan in motion with a patient who ideally fit the criteria. Accepting Doug Sawyer provided a smooth transition from military to civilian for the Ski-Hab staff."

Yeah, sure. A smooth transition for everyone but her.

Good thing Richie wasn't in the same room with her right now. She might have been tempted to strangle him with Ginger's leash. Instead, she gripped the phone tight enough to make her knuckles ache. "Except that he's not just a civilian with an ideal record. He's a reporter. A *sports* reporter."

"Do you even *know* Doug Sawyer, the sports reporter?" he snapped. "Ever read anything he's written?"

"No, but . . ." She hesitated, but on the next breath added,

"What difference does that make? He's a reporter. You know how I feel about—"

"What I know is that you're lumping him in with Lorenzo Akers and all his cockroach pals. And that's not fair to Doug or to you. Maybe once you've read some of his work, you'll understand why I had no qualms about giving him the green light. That's all it took for Kerri-Sue to get onboard."

Ah, yes. Kerri-Sue. Another co-conspirator. "I don't even want to talk about Kerri-Sue except to fire her."

"No one's firing anyone. Not over this. The fact of the matter is, you liked Doug just fine till you found out what he does for a living. Or maybe you just needed the excuse to keep hiding from life."

Her spine snapped to rigid. "What's that supposed to mean?"

"Do your research, Lynnie. *We* did." He hung up before she could form a credible argument.

Never before had she heard that kind of animosity from Richie. Which meant he felt pretty strongly that Doug Sawyer posed no threat to her. Why?

Her shaky legs refused to support her any longer, and she finally had to sink into a cushioned wrought-iron chair near the kitchen's bistro table. She buried her head in her folded arms. After all these years, did Richie really need to be reminded how much she feared the media? Hadn't her flight shown him anything? Or had she run away, not from fear of the media coverage, but as Richie had intimated, from fear of her growing attraction to someone other than Marc? Had she really used Doug's profession as an excuse to flee the man she'd become so fond of?

She sighed. Perhaps Richie was right. She needed more information.

There was a desktop computer in the family room and included in her instructions from Brenda was the password to access the Internet on that machine. Time to find out what Richie knew that she didn't.

Once the computer powered on, she typed "Douglas Sawyer The Sportsman" into the search engine. A long list of entries appeared, including a bibliography of articles written by Douglas Sawyer, sports reporter.

She chose an article at random, "The Trouble with Head Games," and clicked on the related link. The story focused on the proliferation of head injuries and concussions in high school football. Doug had included several case studies from neurologists and trauma doctors, as well as interviews with players, parents, and coaches. The details were thought-provoking. She immediately found herself drawn in to his concerns for the youths who hit the gridiron looking for fun and competition but left injured, sometimes permanently.

She clicked on another article. *Thin Ice* focused on the lives of teenage Olympic skaters in foreign countries, their hardships and sacrifices for their homelands. Memories flooded back to her from her own years on the circuit. As close as her father had kept her, she still had known more freedom than her compatriots from some Eastern European and Asian countries. She and Marc had often wondered what happened to athletes from those places if they failed to bring home a medal. According to what Doug had written about repercussions, their concerns back then were probably well founded.

Lyn read for more than two hours. And in that time, she reconnected with the man under the angel wings. The man who'd awakened her from a decades-long self-imposed exile. Even better, she discovered a reporter who genuinely cared about his subject, whether it was a jockey without health insurance injured in a horse race or the son of a famous athlete trying to crawl out from his father's shadow.

Even his one-on-one interview with a once-famous sports star turned heroin addict and convicted felon portrayed a pitiable man tortured by personal demons. There was no judgment, no chastisement. Just the bare facts about an athlete who'd stumbled and now spent his days reflecting on his former glory while repaying his debt to society.

Every one of Doug's articles featured heart, grit, and the truth behind the not-always-so-glamorous lives of his subjects. He didn't sensationalize his stories, didn't manipulate those he interviewed to make them look foolish or portray them in a bad light. This was the man she'd come to know, the man she'd fallen for. His words reached through the computer to mend the cracks in her heart.

Was it possible she'd misjudged him? That he hadn't simply romanced her for a story? How could she know for sure?

One last article remained, *All Heroes Great and Small.* But the date. The date terrified Lyn. Because this article was printed in *The Sportsman's* online e-zine—surprise!—yesterday. Her index finger tapped aimlessly on the corner of the mouse.

Oh, God. Did she really want to see this?

Yes.

On a sharp intake of breath, she began to read.

Giles Markham sat poised on the brink of mega-stardom. With a Heisman Trophy on his mantel and a Sugar Bowl win on his résumé, he had a bevy of teams ready to launch his professional football career. But Giles chose a different route. At the age of twenty-two, he enlisted in the U.S. Army. After basic training, he hit the ground in some of the fiercest battlegrounds in Iraq. . . .

The article continued, recounting in graphic detail Doug's arrival in Markham's unit, the hardships he and the unit faced, and finally, the fatal Humvee accident.

Lyn's stomach clenched as she read the next few sentences: the laughter seconds before the explosion, the Humvee's tumble, and the silent blackness Doug experienced. Knowing him so well, she sensed the pain he must have felt as he told of waking up in a foreign hospital, surrounded by strangers, hooked up to machines that beeped and blinked and terrified him. She burst into tears again; this time she wept *for* Doug, not because of him.

. . . If not for some very dedicated people, that might have been the end of my story—and my life. But I was lucky. Without my knowledge, or even my cooperation, family and friends enrolled me in Ski-Hab, a program for disabled soldiers. There, I met a host of new heroes. . . .

Although he used no names, Doug managed to clearly convey the personalities of each of his classmates, the members of the therapy team, and Kerri-Sue through colorful narrative and affectionate nicknames like Lance Corporal Bride-to-Be and PFC Future Lawyer. He even included a full rundown on the founder's past military and rehabilitation history, then concluded with the town's desire to give back to their first Gulf War hero. He overlooked no one. Well, almost no one.

In fact, one person remained conspicuously absent from his detailed article. Her.

Of course, her cynical brain reminded her, he might have simply edited out all details that referenced her after what had happened at Richie's house. A cold wetness hit her elbow, and she flinched, then looked down at Ginger's warm brown eyes.

"You're thinking I'm selling him short, aren't you?" She scratched Ginger behind the ears. The dog, naturally, said nothing, but she lay her chin on Lyn's lap. "I don't suppose you know what my next move should be, do you?"

Ginger didn't utter a sound.

On a sigh, Lyn stood. "God, I'm losing my mind." The clock on the far wall glowed 6:58 P.M. Time for her daily press monitoring. The seven o'clock gossip shows were about to start.

She dragged herself away from the computer and turned back to Ginger. "You coming?"

The dog, now lying on the terra-cotta tile floor, placed her head on her front paws.

"Okay," Lyn said. "Your loss."

She picked up the remote control, turned on the television, then flipped to the channel she needed. A popular muckraker popped on the screen in full HDTV. Once she settled on the couch, she managed to sit through twenty minutes of airhead journalism and inane commercials with no tense moments. Thank God. The furor was dying down. Soon she could go home.

The idea, however, didn't thrill her the way it should. What did she have to go home to? A nice business, a gossipy neighbor, a few ski runs in the winter.

Alone. Always alone.

She cast a glance at Ginger. She'd miss her new friend. Maybe, when she finally did go home, she'd look into a greyhound rescue of her own. She'd have to do the research first, make sure the idea was feasible in a bed-and-breakfast. How would a greyhound react to a steady stream of strangers?

"And finally, tonight," the show's blond, vapid host said, "from the 'Where in the World Are the Raine Girls?' file, we caught up with April and Dr. Jeff in Manhattan, shopping for the perfect wedding venue...."

The gossip show cut away from the studio to breezy city streets where April snuggled against Jeff and answered questions shouted out from passersby. A gaggle of microphones bounced near her face, but she never lost her step or faltered. The whole scene was ludicrous. April drew the crowds, reeled them in with romantic looks and lots of giggles.

To keep them far away from where Lyn hid here in this house.

Thank you, April.

Always the brave one, her older sister. Unlike Lyn, who huddled here like a scared rabbit. Or a coward.

What had happened to Brooklyn Raine? Where was the woman who'd conquered mountains all over the world? Had she really become so timid?

April's advice ran through her head once again. *You don't just take a chance when you play Monopoly, kiddo.*

And you couldn't find love in games of solitaire either.

Suddenly, Lyn knew exactly what she wanted. She just had to find the courage to take the chance.

Chapter Twenty-one

Early the next morning, Lyn sat in the kitchen, a cup of coffee to her left and a bowl of rough-cut oatmeal on her right. For about the hundredth time so far, her focus strayed to the numerals glowing orange on the stainless steel microwave. Not quite seven o'clock. Still too early to call Brenda. She tapped a teaspoon against her cup. *Tink-tink-tink.*

Ginger, curled into a canine comma against the bank of cabinets, jerked up her head.

"Sorry," Lyn whispered to the greyhound. "Go back to sleep. It's too early to be awake yet."

But, of course, Ginger didn't speak English. All she knew was that the human was up and she was up. Therefore, it must be time for a walk. She unfolded her long legs and stood, then trotted to the utility closet. One glance at Lyn, then a glance at the closed door before she sat and waited. Another glance. More waiting.

Lyn resisted for a full five minutes before the dog's soulful pleading eyes finally proved too much. "Well." She gave an exaggerated sigh and rose slowly to her feet. "It's not like I can call Brenda yet, anyway. Let's do it, girl."

As if the dog understood, she leaped to her feet, grin wide and long pink tongue lolling. Lyn strode to the closet to grab the leash. While Ginger pranced around her, she slipped into her coat. With the leash clamped on the dog's collar, they exited the house.

Dawn tinged the gray eastern sky with ribbons of mauve. Morning temperatures, barely above freezing, made puffy clouds from her breath as Ginger led her in a gallop around the neighborhood. She used the solitude to jump-start her brain and review her plan. So many variables, so many things that could go wrong. Adrenaline dripped into her veins, tingling her skin and energizing her mind. She'd make this work, cover every angle, face the challenge, take the chance.

When they returned to the townhouse, Lyn hung up her coat and stowed the leash, then strode into the kitchen. And paused in front of the microwave. The clock glowed 8:58 A.M. Really? They'd been gone for an hour? Apparently, she'd been so absorbed in her thoughts, she'd completely lost track of time.

The upside? She could now call Brenda. After fixing a fresh cup of coffee for caffeinated fortitude, she picked up the cell phone, found Brenda in the contacts list—not too difficult since she was the only number listed—and hit the green PHONE button to connect her call. Two rings went by.

"Thank you for calling Rainey-Day-Wife. How can I make your burden easier today?"

Easier? Hardly. Lyn's burden was about to become Herculean. "Brenda? It's Lyn. Brooklyn. April's sister?" God, she sounded like a moron.

"Lyn? Everything okay?"

"Yeah." For the next three seconds or so. After that, well, the jury was out. She swallowed her fear and plowed on. "I've been thinking, and I know this is last minute. I hope it's okay. But . . ." The words came out in a rush. "Iwanttogohome."

Brenda sucked in a breath sharp enough to pierce Lyn's eardrum. "Oh, sweetie, I'm not sure that's such a good idea. I mean, April's doing a great job of keeping the press occupied, but the reporters are still hanging around outside your inn. You show up now—"

"I show up now, and they're going to have to deal with me." The words came out strong and sure. *You go, girl.* "Bren, I know April told you to take care of me and, honestly, I'm grateful. But it's time for me to stop hiding. From the press, from life." From love. But she kept that last one to herself. "The only thing that worries me is that I know this totally screws you up with Ginger, and I'm sorry."

"Don't be," Brenda replied with a chuckle. "Ginger's regular caregiver will be thrilled to have her back. But are you sure?"

"Yes."

"Looks like I owe your sister ten bucks."

Lyn traced a finger in the gray-swirled pattern of the marble tabletop. "What do you mean?"

"She said love would wake you up. She's right, isn't she? You're in love?"

A thrill raced through her blood. Love. Was it love? This fuzzy, upside-down feeling? The reason her thoughts flew to Doug a thousand times a day? The eagerness to see him, touch him, to simply be near him? "Yes."

"Hooray! Go get him, Lynnie. You deserve your happiness. But be careful. Keep the cell phone with you. Same rules apply there as they do here. If you need anything, call. Even from miles away, I've been known to work a miracle or two in my time."

Maybe. But this miracle, Lyn had to achieve on her own.

Lyn drove up the long, winding driveway that led to Snowed Inn. Butterflies danced in her stomach, only partly due to the proliferation of news vans parked along the side of the road. She counted two local, two national, and one cable entertainment network among the chaos. Another reason for her flutters came from a more pleasant source, the rush of the unknown. She'd faced down a lot of challengers in her day, but today she intended to slay the beast and win her prince. If he'd let her.

She pulled into the parking area and turned off the engine. The minute she stepped out of the car, the horde surged forward. Lights flashed and microphones popped up in her face from every angle.

"Brooklyn! Where've you been?"

"Brooklyn, is it true you're having an affair with Ace Riordan?"

"Did you and April have a fight? Is that why she left so suddenly?"

"Just a few words, Brooklyn, please? For the fans?"

She ignored them all, holding her arm out straight to keep

them a fair distance away as she sped to her front porch. Reaching the door with the cranberry wreath, she quickly turned the handle. Nothing happened.

Locked. And she had no keys with her.

"You could try knocking," a man in the crowd suggested.

"But no one's answered in days."

Guffaws of laughter erupted from the throng while heat scalded Lyn's cheeks. *Okay, don't panic.* On a sharp intake of breath, she fisted her hand, prepared to knock.

The door slipped open a sliver, and Mrs. Bascomb's eyeball appeared. "Lyn. Thank God. Hurry. Get inside before these vultures start squawking."

"They're already squawking." Lyn slipped inside through the miniscule crack Mrs. Bascomb had opened, then quickly shut and locked the door again. Pausing by the small round table with the pot of African violets, she removed her gloves.

Home. She breathed in the scents of cinnamon and cider, a hint of wood smoke. Each bit of familiarity strengthened her resolve, helped assure her of victory. She *could* do this.

"Thank goodness that nice Brenda called me to say you were on your way home. I've been watching for you for hours now. Where did you go? And why are you back so soon?"

"Later," Lyn said with a dismissive wave of her hand. "Right now, I have to make a phone call."

"Yes, but before you do—"

"Later," Lyn repeated, slapping her leather gloves on the tabletop with force. "This is important."

"But you should know—"

One fierce look and Mrs. Bascomb backed down. Thank God. Because Lyn was fired up enough to incinerate.

Without removing her coat or hat, she sped straight to the phone in the sitting room and punched in the number for information. Anxiety kept her hopping, shifting her weight from one foot to the other. When the operator gave her the option, she chose to splurge on the extra twenty-five cents to have the call connected for her automatically, rather than risk misdialing thanks to her jittery nerves.

The silence seemed to go on for several minutes, but it was

probably mere seconds before the phone clicked and the ringing began.

She barely allowed the receptionist to utter the complex's name before she blurted, "Douglas Sawyer's room, please."

"One moment, please," the receptionist intoned, then clicked her to the annoying music on hold. An updated version of "Quando, Quando, Quando." *Tell me, when will you be mine?* How fitting.

"Lyn." Like a mosquito in the dark, Mrs. Bascomb buzzed around her again. "I think you should know—"

Oh, for heaven's sake. She turned her back on the old woman. Rude, but so was Mrs. Bascomb's continued interruptions. She needed no distractions right now. Not when she was about to take this giant leap of faith.

With a click, the receptionist came back on the phone. "I'm sorry, ma'am, but Mr. Sawyer checked out a few days ago."

"Oh." Excitement drained from her in a flood. She sank to the floor, her back braced against the wall to keep from crumpling in a heap. "My mistake. Thank you."

Oh, God. Too late. She'd missed him. Desolation swept over her. Folding her still-jacketed arms over her head, she curled into a ball. *Okay, deep breaths, Lyn. This isn't the end of the race; it's just a mogul field. You can regroup. You'll call Ace. Get Doug's number. You can still make this work.*

"Lyn?" His voice reached through her protective shell, and she jerked up to see him kneeling beside her, those marvelous eyes shining with concern. "You okay?"

"Doug?" She blinked. It couldn't be. People didn't just magically appear because you wished them to. But he *was* real. He really was here. She struggled to rise, her legs shaking too violently to complete the effort.

Until Doug reached a hand to help. His *right* hand, she noted. Joy overwhelmed her, and she flung her arms around his neck. The thick padding of her ski jacket prevented the closeness she craved, but other concerns took priority at the moment. "What are you doing here?"

He shrugged as he released her. "I had to check out of the condo at Andiron."

"Because of what I said at Richie's?" Guilt warmed her cheeks, and she cast her gaze to the floor. "Oh, God, Doug. I'm sorry. I couldn't be more sorry."

"Don't be. You were right."

Her jaw dropped. "I was?"

"Yeah. Look, why don't you take off your coat and hat? Eleanor can get us some hot cider and cookies—she says you like that in the afternoon. The cider's a bit sweet for me, but if it makes you happy, I'm willing to drink cider. The cookies are pretty good though. Gerta made gingersnaps yesterday. I haven't had those since I was a kid. It's no wonder your inn is so popular. A person could get spoiled by your staff."

Her head spun while she tried to keep up with his rambling. Finally, she grabbed him by the arms. "Doug, slow down. I'm still trying to get used to the idea you're in my inn."

"If you'd let me get a word in," Mrs. Bascomb harrumphed from the doorway, "I would have told you he's been staying here since you took off."

She veered her attention from Doug to Mrs. Bascomb and then back to Doug. "You have?"

Another shrug. "Take off your coat, and we'll sit in the parlor like civilized people and talk. Okay?"

"Okay." After pulling her wool cap off her head, she unzipped her jacket. Rather than waste time and risk losing contact with Doug, she quickly peeled off her outer garments and tossed them onto the Queen Anne chair near the phone. "All set."

Taking Doug's hand, she pulled him into the parlor at a near run.

He laughed. "Easy, Lyn, slow down. I'm not going anywhere."

"Yeah, well, I'm not willing to take that chance."

"Oh?" He stopped and looked down at her, eyes narrowed in scrutiny. "And what brought about this change?"

"Later." To prompt him to continue, she perched in the love seat near the fireplace and patted the empty cushion beside her. "You go first. How did you wind up here?"

Following her lead, he sat. "Well, like I said, I couldn't stay at the Andiron since I was no longer participating in Ski-Hab. But I had an article to write."

She held up a hand. "About that—"

"Later." He took her fingers, squeezed, then dropped their linked hands between them. "I'm first, remember? So, anyway, I needed to continue research for my article. And all my research was best done here, where the main characters lived. After I checked out of the Andiron, I asked my cab driver for the name of the best inn in town. He brought me to Snowed Inn, of course."

Relaxing against him, she smirked. "Don't tell me. Let me guess. Larry?"

He wrapped his left arm around her, holding her close. "Is he the only cab driver in town?"

"Believe it or not, no." She snuggled into his embrace while the fire and his presence warmed her. "But if the fare has anything to do with me, Larry makes himself available. And since he knows you're sweet on me . . ." She lifted an eyebrow in Doug's direction.

"Sweet on you, huh? That's what this feeling is?"

Embarrassment heated her cheeks. "Would that be such a bad thing?"

His fingers propped up her chin, and his gaze locked on her face. "If I thought that, I wouldn't be here now."

"Are you saying your research wasn't the only reason you stayed here?"

He traced a finger down her jawline, softly, gently. "I might have hoped to see you again."

A thrill rippled through her. "I read your article. It's one of the reasons I came back."

The finger paused at the tender skin behind her earlobe. "Oh?"

"Yes. I was thinking that maybe. . . ." Her courage faltered, and she stared into the dancing flames in the fireplace.

"Maybe . . . ?" he prompted.

"I thought, maybe, you might want to write another article. This time, about me."

"No, I don't think so."

She sat up and stared at him aghast. "No? Why on earth not?"